I0606743

Necessary Stories

Necessary Stories

Necessary Stories

Haim Watzman

West 26th Street Press
New York

Copyright 2017 by Haim Watzman

All rights reserved. Printed in the United States of America. No part of this book may be used or reproduced in any manner whatsoever without written permission, except for brief quotations embodied in critical articles and reviews.

For permissions and reprint rights, please write to the author, hwatzman@gmail.com

These stories, with the exception of "Possession," first appeared, in slightly different forms, in *The Jerusalem Report* and on the Southjerusalem.com website.
First edition

Cover design by Mizmor Watzman
Cover illustration by Avi Katz

For Niot, who left too soon.

Contents

An Unnecessary Introduction

Etymologically, there's no connection between the words *story* and *store*. Or at least that's what my dictionary tells me. *Story*, meaning a tale, is a word from Middle English deriving from the Latin *historia*, while *store*, referring to a stock or supply set aside for future use, comes from the Old French *estore*, meaning provisions.

That these words are unrelated makes no sense to me. What is a story, after all, but a quantum of life—real, remembered, imagined—set aside for future use?

True, one might argue that the two things have nothing in common. A *provision* – the meaning of that word is hidden in plain sight—is a looking forward, while a *story* is a looking backwards, but Haim Watzman's *Necessary Stories*, the collection you now hold in your hands, is an argument against that.

Watzman's quiet greatness as a writer is, in fact, that he understands there is no contradiction here at all.

Life, as we know only too well, is fleeting. Our childhoods, our youths, the people who came before us, sometimes the people who come after us, everything we know and everything we experience—it all disappears in the rearview mirror as we hurtle faster and faster towards our ultimate destination. Our lives, for the most part, are lived and forgotten, and a vast amount of our day-to-day experiences, falling through the cracks of memory, makes no lasting impression on us at all.

Or rather not until a writer like Watzman decides to put a little bit of it aside for future use—as a story, as a store, as a necessary provision.

"Here," he seems to be saying to us. "Hold onto this. Hold onto this little moment. You might just need it in the future."

There are many lives and many worlds described in this vast storyteller's warehouse of tales. There are personal narratives, family stories, historical monologues, tales of Talmudic or biblical magic realism. There are fantasies and literary scherzos, shaggy dog stories, realistic accounts of contemporary American and Israeli life. A sweetness runs through the collection, binding its disparate parts, and a sense of sadness, too, both of which, I think, come from Watzman's deep and softly felt understanding that the small lives we all lead, filled with small people and small events, are nevertheless experienced by us as though we were all characters in a Wagnerian opera cycle.

Watzman knows that every encounter, no matter how fleeting—a conversation in a cemetery with a long-dead Talmudic sage; Felix Mendelssohn's great aunt scolding the young prodigy; four Jews on a plane discussing the Bible, the Zohar and *Wuthering Heights*—is a matter of life and death.

Necessary Stories is a quietly beautiful work, haunting in places, gently funny in others, written by a graceful, thoughtful, eloquent man who understands that life itself is not enough. One must live to tell the tale.

Joseph Skibell
Tesuque, NM
November 2016

Author's Introduction

Some months after my second book, *A Crack in the Earth*, came out in 2007, I was approached by Eetta Price-Gibson, who had recently been appointed editor of a biweekly Israeli news magazine, *The Jerusalem Report*. She made a tempting offer—two pages, once every four weeks, to fill with pretty much whatever I wanted.

The pay was not great, but the opportunity was tempting. After long years as a journalist and translator, I felt the itch to try my hand at something new. I suggested the name "Necessary Stories" for the column—the name I had originally wished to give my memoir *Company C*, but which the publisher nixed as being too uninformative about the content of a book about my experiences in the Israel Defense Forces reserves.

I'd spent my life up to then writing short newspaper and magazine pieces and translating non-fiction books from Hebrew into English. From the time I began supporting myself, I investigated, researched, interviewed, and then reported what I learned in the clearest and most objective way I could. While my two books also involved research, and both were based on fact, they also gave me a chance to play with narrative, develop characters, convey mood, and at times to favor ambiguity over direct exposition. I found myself following the example of the writers I like best, those who challenge their audiences by leaving holes in their stories for readers to fill in. Most of all,

I best like those books that leave me feeling, when I reach their ends, that I urgently need to read them once more. It was that kind of writing I wanted to do.

The early installments were in the form of personal essays, along with some political satire. It took me a while to find my voice, to loosen up enough to stop feeling like my job was to report about other people rather than to write from my own heart. The essays grew more personal, more indirect, more literary. It was fun, but I wasn't satisfied. I realized that I didn't want to just write about myself, or about real people and events. I wanted to make people up, and imagine what they did. The editors resisted at first, but soon I was writing the oddest of things—a fiction column in a news magazine.

That wouldn't have been so unusual a generation ago, when most general magazines published short fiction. Today's short story writers, if they get their work out at all, generally publish in literary magazines, where they enjoy small audiences made up mostly of other writers. Publishing in *The Jerusalem Report*, I'm off the radar of the literary world but have the opportunity to be read by people who don't normally read short stories nor seek them out in specialized venues. Also, I actually get paid to write fiction, a rare privilege in these times.

I've been writing the column for nine years now; early in 2016 I published story number 100. About once a month I get an email from a stranger who's read and liked a piece, or I get accosted on the street or at the pool or at synagogue by an acquaintance or unfamiliar face who, I am delighted to discover, is a regular reader. I don't think a writer can ask for more than that. Sometimes they ask whether there is a *Necessary Stories* book; until now I've had no choice but to shrug and reply that, no, there isn't.

The real impetus for putting this collection together came last year at the biannual Sami Rohr Jewish Literary Institute, a forum I'm privileged to be invited to. A number of the other writers asked why I hadn't done a collection. I said that I would never do so unless a top-flight editor went through the stories to help me polish and improve them. And, I told them, being a top-flight editor myself, I know how much one costs, and I can't afford it. To my surprise, Joseph Skibell, a gifted novelist and essayist, stepped into the breach. He volunteered his eye and his red pen, and over the months that followed he read through the stories I chose and made myriad suggestions that have vastly improved my work. I am incredibly grateful to him.

Once the stories were in final form, a consortium of friends and readers volunteered to proofread them. I'm grateful to all of them: Asher Arbit, Yitzhak Avigad, Sara Avitzour, George Eltman, Ari Goldman, Linda Gradstein, Avi Hoffman, Renee Melammed, Jessica Cohen, Austin Ratner, Mindy Schimmel, and my sister, Nancy Watzman.

The appearance of this book would also not have been possible had my agent, Simon Lipskar of Writers House, not suggested that, in today's publishing world, I'd be better off putting this book out on my own rather than seeking a publisher. Writers House has done something wonderful for its writers in setting up a mechanism for doing this easily and inexpensively with the agency's help and involvement. Julie Trelstad and Daniel Berkowitz, the digital directors, and Celia Taylor Mobley, Simon's assistant, have been hugely helpful in getting this done.

The stories before you, with one exception, were published in *The Jerusalem Report* and, by prior arrangement, on my website, South Jerusalem, where readers can find a complete archive. ("Possession," too long for the magazine, has been waiting for this opportunity.) I'm grateful to the editors of the magazine over the years—Eetta Price Gibson, Matthew Kalman, Avi Hoffman, and Ilan Evyatar—for the pages they've offered me and their enthusiasm for the stories, and to the rest of the staff for catching typos, infelicities, and inconsistencies.

Avi Katz has illustrated most of the stories on behalf of *The Jerusalem Report*. In the tradition of the great illustrators of the past, his work adds a dimension of its own. I'm lucky to have his collaboration. A few of his best appear here; others can be seen on my website.

Jane Golbert and Annabelle Landgarten, my partners in "The Necessary Stories Show," a staged version of some of these tales, have also had valuable suggestions and insights.

My daughter Mizmor, a talented artist and animator, designed the cover and has helped out in many other ways.

Without the encouragement, support, and stability provided by the rest of my family—my older son Asor and his wife Adi, my younger daughter Misgav, and most importantly my wife Ilana—none of these stories would have been written. My younger son, Niot, a soldier in the Golani Brigade, was felled in a diving accident during the Pesach holiday in 2011. His loss has shaped the content and tone of everything I have written since. We all continue to miss him intensely. This book is dedicated to his memory.

Haim Watzman
Jerusalem
November 2016

PART I: THE BEST IT CAN BE

The Importance of Low Expectations

I remember a high wind and driving rain. Night is darker here, I thought, as the bus's engine expired in a series of knocks that sounded like the final beats of a broken heart. We pulled our duffle bags and backpacks from the luggage compartment and dragged them in the direction of the faintly-lit doorway of the Kiryat Shmonah Absorption Center, which was to be our home and our school for the next three months. The only effect of the buzz and bluster of the other young people was to make me feel more alone, unanchored in a new land. Isolation, though raw, was my medium; I had expected nothing more.

I was not the first to feel alone here. "Only once in his life can a person arrive in the Land of Israel for the first time," wrote Yehuda Ya'ari, one of the literary lights of the idealistic, ideological Third Aliya, with regret and, probably, considerable remorse. Ya'ari, who abandoned his socialist kibbutz paradise early on and parted from his utopian comrades, was still alive, and living in Jerusalem, when I arrived in the Land of Israel that October night three decades ago. At that time I knew nothing of him, but today, nearly forty years later, as I think back on that night, his words resonate.

There were twenty-eight of us in the commons room of the absorption center, waiting to be assigned our rooms. Damp spots stained the corners of the ceiling, where the rain was seeping through, and the plaster was cracked. A telephone—one of the handful of telephones in the entire town—stood on the reception desk at one end of the room, firmly locked.

Shy as I was, I'd made some initial acquaintances on the four-hour ride up from the airport in Lod. The group was made up mostly of Americans, but there were a handful of Brits and Canadians and one easygoing Australian. A girl from New York was religious; two, one guy and one woman, weren't even Jewish. I was one of only seven men, meaning that for each one of us there were three women. Whatever hopes I had, however, were soon dashed as I watched the women's eyes gravitate to the Australian, who was the tallest of us, and to the non-Jew, who was by far the best-looking. I got into a political debate with a woman with close-cropped, jet-black hair and dark eyes, and was taken by the sharpness of her mind and the unconventionality of her thinking. But then she told me she was a lesbian. The other women laughed and chattered on the bus, but they seemed to talk to me from behind a barrier. Most of them announced that they had serious boyfriends at home to whom they intended to remain loyal over the course of the year. When I expressed skepticism about their simple faith, they dismissed me.

Another interesting statistic had emerged on the bus. Seven of the twenty-eight—the Australian among them—declared that they had come on aliya. They were Zionist idealists who intended to spend the rest of their lives in Israel. Fourteen others were open to the idea. The remaining seven—I was one of these—were certain that we had come for a year and had no desire at all to make Israel our permanent home. All of us were enrolled in Sherut La'am, a program sponsored by the Jewish Agency, in which we would spend three months learning Hebrew in Israel's northernmost and most beleaguered urban center and then disperse to development towns across the country, to do what we could, as untrained volunteers, to help these poor and neglected communities. My plan was to do my duty to the Jewish people reconstituted in their nation-state, and then go home. That the duty was difficult and lonely made it feel all the more real and important.

It was 1978 and I'd graduated from college the previous May; I was one of the youngest members of the group. Also, I was a relative novice when it came to experience in Israel. It was only my second trip; most of my fellow volunteers had been several times, in many cases for extended periods, living on kibbutzim or in one of the big cities. A large percentage had been active during high school and college in Zionist youth groups. For them, Israel was almost a second home; for me it intrigued precisely because it was foreign, murky, and forbidding. I was young; suffering and hardship were the path that I had learned to use to get inside myself.

I'd made my first trip two winters previously, a quick two-week tour in the company of a group of extremely unpleasant Long Island college students. They were strangers to me—we'd been thrown together after the trip I originally signed up for fell through. Nevertheless, their interminable bitching didn't keep me from seeing the sights and becoming curious enough to want to come back. But certainly not to stay.

It was Hol HaMo'ed, the intermediate days of the Sukkot holiday, when we arrived—a fact of which I was vaguely aware, even though Sukkot was not a holiday my family had ever paid much attention to. As we dripped in the commons room, we were told that the country was on vacation, and that we'd be set free the next day to go wherever we wished until our Hebrew studies commenced after Simhat Torah. Too exhausted to complain, my emotions sequestered, unable to ask what I was supposed to do and where I was supposed to go, I heaved my duffel bag up to my room and fell asleep.

"Had they shown us such a Galilee in a dream," Ya'ari wrote in his 1937 novel *Like Glittering Light*, "our souls would have ached with yearning and longing for it; now that it revealed itself to us face to face, in reality, our souls were in awful anguish." Perhaps Ya'ari was recalling his first dawn in Beit Alfa, then a lonely outpost at the eastern end of the Jezre'el Valley. But when I rose to look out over the Hula Valley the next morning, I'd had no dreams that could be shattered. A mist, coaxed out of the green fields before me by the rising sun, broke the early morning rays and made it seem as if I were seeing the Galilean landscape through a crystal ball. The Golan Heights looked like a mossy embankment close enough to touch, and just to the northeast the Hermon rose into a bank of clouds that, I imagined, were grooming and dressing the mountain for the day before it. Behind me, the Menara cliff face provided a rich brown backdrop to the homes and housing projects of Kiryat Shmonah, which insisted on looking peaceful and pastoral, even if katyusha rockets and terrorists sometimes came over the mountain from Lebanon to wreak havoc in the town.

I threw a spare pair of jeans and a couple shirts into my backpack and headed with the others up the street to the Kiryat Shmonah bus terminal. Many of the volunteers were going to spend the long weekend before us with family; others were heading off, unannounced, to the kibbutzim where they'd formerly spent summers or semesters, knowing that they'd be welcomed warmly. All I had was a scrap of paper with the name and address of cousins of a friend of mine who, he had assured me, would be delighted to host me whenever I could get to Jerusalem.

The scrap of paper led me to a small street just off King George in the capital; three flights up a narrow and dusky staircase I knocked on a door. The thin and unshaven man who opened it smiled when I introduced myself. "We were expecting you," he said, even though I'd had no way of informing them that I was coming. I had a place to stay and some Israelis to observe.

Yesterday's refreshing rain had now turned into a fierce heat wave. The small apartment was stuffy. Even with my twenty-two-year old male blindness to disarray, I could see that the rooms had not been cleaned any time recently. A small girl, perhaps three years old and clothed only from the waist up, was running and shouting among cast-off toys and discarded slices of bread. A voice called out a greeting from an inner room. "It's my wife," my host said. "She is nine months pregnant and can't get up."

Perhaps I should go, I suggested. We will not hear of it, he replied, seconded loudly by his wife and his daughter.

He took me out to the Sukkah on their tiny balcony and asked me if I would like to say the blessing on the lulav and etrog. I would and I did, for the first time in my life. That evening we attended Friday night services in a crowded Hasidic shteibel and returned home to dine on boiled chicken and potatoes. My host made up the couch for me in the dark. I'd never before been a guest in Jerusalem; if this was the city's customary hospitality, it seemed good enough to me. A bit strange, perhaps, but challenging, different, and interesting.

A commotion disturbed me briefly in the middle of the night; someone whispered something about my keeping an eye on the little girl. I nodded and fell back into a deep sleep. The next morning my host woke me up. "I have a son," he said happily.

"They were all young—of the generation of the war," Ya'ari wrote in his story "What He Had Not Yet Told Her." "A great terror was in their hearts, the terror of war, and in their souls an ambition for redemption, redemption of the nation and redemption of humanity. And I'll tell you a secret: this ambition was much larger than they could contain or conceive. A huge need in a soul that is not so large can make a man lose his mind."

Three days later, the morning after Simhat Torah, I boarded the 963 bus and watched from the window as rusty signs pointed down to Jericho, up the Bik'a Valley, through Beit She'an, around Lake Kinneret, via Tiberias, up to Kiryat Shmonah. I stood most of the way; the bus was full of soldiers returning to their bases after the holiday. Despite the open windows, the air in the bus was dense with heat, damp with humidity, and smoky from the soldiers' cigarettes.

I didn't have much of a vocabulary, but in Hebrew school I'd been that peculiar and rare sort of student who loved grammar. As I knew my conjugations, I was placed in the highest level Hebrew class, taught by Yitzhak, a multi-lingual elder who'd come from Holland in the late thirties to help found a kibbutz nearby.

"It was very tough. Many grew disappointed and disillusioned," he told us. "But I wasn't like most of the others. I hadn't dreamed of being a pioneer in Palestine and came almost by chance. So the experience far exceeded the very low expectations I'd arrived with. Perhaps that is the secret of a successful aliya."

To the best of my knowledge, of the seven declared olim in our group, only one remains today. And I, who swore I was here for a year and no more, am now not far from celebrating the fortieth anniversary of my aliya. Yehuda Ya'ari knew the anguish of broken dreams; my teacher Yitzhak knew the value of having no dreams at all. My heart was small then, I think. Looking back, I wonder whether it was not perhaps for the best that I didn't try to cram dreams and love into it. Life, and Israel, were far from paradise in the autumn of 1978. But they were good enough, and there was no disappointment.

The Devil and Theodor Herzl

Herzl adjusted his mouse-gray gloves and followed the young secretary through a massive door. The secretary had a well-trimmed beard that gave him a strong resemblance to the czar.

"Mr. Herzl, Your Excellency," the secretary announced, standing as stiff as a sentry at a military tomb.

The man at the desk penned notes in the margins of a document. His desk testified to the assiduousness and deliberateness of his character. Dossiers and documents were piled high on the interior minister's left, a large brass telephone stood at his right hand. In front of him, partly blocking Herzl's view of his host's head, were the gilded accouterments of a high imperial official—two tall candlesticks, two inkwells, a paperweight in the shape of a crouching lion, a triumphant angel that served, it seemed, as a pen stand. All were carefully polished; they glinted in the dappled August sunlight that filtered in through the oak outside a north-facing bay window. Behind the desk hung a large portrait of Czar Alexander III and a smaller icon of St. Mary Magdalene. Herzl felt faint, his beard itched, he steeled himself. This meeting might be a huge step toward securing, for the first time, a great power's commitment to the establishment of a Jewish state. Or it might compromise him irreparably, and impel his associates in the movement he had founded to depose him.

"I believe Mr. Herzl would appreciate a breeze," the man at the desk said in French, his face still close to the page he was writing on.

The secretary strode over and opened the window. The minister of the interior looked up approvingly, revealing a bushy gray mustache. Taking in a deep breath, he stabbed his pen into the angel's back. Then he offered his guest the smile of a much younger man, one who was planning some mischief as soon as the adults got out of the way. He looked more like an uncle who liked to romp on the living room floor with his nieces and nephews than Vyacheslav von Plehve, the brutal repressor of rebellions and hangman of revolutionaries.

"That will do," he said to the secretary, who nodded and withdrew. Plehve came around the desk and took Herzl's hand in both of his.

"Herr Herzl," he said. "Baroness von Suttner has told me so much about you. I feel we have a great deal in common. Please sit down." He motioned to the large plush chair facing his desk and then, almost comically, bounded back into his own throne-like seat.

Suddenly serious, von Plehve clasped his hands before him on his desk. "First, allow me to convey to you, as the leader of the Jewish people, my Imperial Majesty's most profound regret at the unfortunate events in Kishinev this past Easter. His Majesty is saddened by the loss of so many of his Jewish subjects and those who have been left injured and without homes, all as the result of a most regrettable misunderstanding."

Herzl repressed his body's desire to jerk. Control was everything. Good German control could win out over Slavic emotionalism. But then he, a Jew from Budapest, was about as German as von Plehve, a Baltic Teuton, was a Russian. They were probably evenly matched. "Your sentiments, and those of his Imperial Majesty," he told his host, putting an ever-so-mild tinge of sarcasm in his voice, "are most gratefully received."

Plehve's voice took on a harsher tone. His eyes flashed. "But his Imperial Majesty has also asked me to inform you how wounded he is by the attacks on him and his government, most specifically on his minister of the interior, by the Jewish and international press—which, as we know, is much the same thing. The Jews accuse him of instigating, encouraging, and not doing all in his power to end the disturbances."

Herzl offered a smile of his own, and not the obsequious one that the czar's interior minister might have expected from the leader of a miniscule national movement with no legions, no territory, and few resources. Perhaps the Ancient of Days, or Clio, the muse of history, had craftily arranged to make the leader of the fledgling Zionist Organization a leading member of the one profession that the minister truly feared—a journalist. Plehve had made the mistake of revealing his Achilles heel from the start.

"I believe that His Excellency will see the press's attitude change if he is forthcoming on the issues presented in my memorandum."

Plehve leaned back in his chair and surveyed the man in front of him. "I have asked you to come see me so that we might reach an understanding with you about the Zionist movement, of which you are the leader." He thought a moment. "The nature of the relationship which will be established between the Imperial Government and Zionism—and which can become, I will not say amicable, but let us say proper—will depend on you."

Herzl nodded.

Plehve quickly added: "I should stress that the Jewish question is not a vital issue for us. But it is one for which we have no solution at present. On the one hand, the Russian state is bound to desire the homogeneity of its population. At the very least, we demand of all the peoples in our empire, and therefore also of the Jews, that they act as Russian patriots. As patriots, they may assimilate into the Russian people through higher education and economic advancement, though of course we must restrict their numbers in our universities and government service so that we do not run out of places for Christians."

"I can assure you that all my Russian Zionist colleagues are loyal subjects of the czar," Herzl said, "and engage in no activity opposed to their emperor or his government."

"Indeed," Plehve said. "I should point out that some do not share my admiration for your people. At a recent meeting of the cabinet, my esteemed friend, the minister of finance, told our Imperial Majesty that he would be quite happy if it were possible to drown Russia's six million Jews in the Black Sea. I do not share that view. I believe that we must give the Jews an opportunity to live. Indeed, I understand their position. If I were a Jew, I believe I would also be attracted to the revolutionaries."

"More than they are rebelling, they are fleeing," Herzl noted.

Plehve nodded. "Our problem, indeed, is that while the French and English berate us for being cruel tyrants, they themselves have become alarmed at the numbers of Jews entering their countries and are passing laws to staunch the flow. This means that dissatisfied and frightened Jews will remain here and join the Social Revolutionaries.

"At the same time, the bad press that Russia has received has made it very difficult for His Imperial Majesty to obtain the loans he needs to maintain order and to pursue his interests in the Far East."

Plehve tapped his pen on his desk. "Therefore, the creation of an independent Jewish state, capable of absorbing several million Jews, would suit us."

"I have noted in my memorandum a number of steps that His Imperial Majesty's government could take to further our program," Herzl said. "If he will personally intervene with the sultan, allow our movement to promote emigration to Palestine, and take certain steps to ameliorate the poverty and oppression of the Jews in Russia, I have every reason to believe that governments and banks in the West will view with favor Russia's requests for credit."

Plehve stroked his mustache. "You bargain as well as a Turk in a bazaar," he said. "Of course, you people learn that from a young age."

Herzl did not reply.

The interior minister took a large dossier from the left side of his desk, placed it carefully in the middle, and opened it up.

"You are a brave man," he said, "to negotiate with a man your people see as a criminal."

"I have no reason to doubt that His Excellency works solely for the welfare and security of the czar's subjects," Herzl replied.

Plehve turned over page after page in the dossier.

"Many of your colleagues are angry with you for meeting me," he said. "You know of course that we are fully informed about the most intimate discussions of the Russian Zionists. Among your colleagues are some who are quite happy to provide us with detailed reports. Although it would, of course, be very embarrassing for them if I were to reveal their names."

"His Excellency is renowned for his extensive knowledge," Herzl said.

"They say that you betray your people and your movement by shaking the hand of the Butcher of Kishinev. How can a man claiming to represent the Jewish people exchange pleasantries with the man who, at the very least, did not send troops in to stop the rioting, who let it go on for three full days without interference? This at a time when the bodies of the dead are still warm, the widows and orphans still mourning their dead, the homeless still roaming the streets, the young women still heavy with the issue of the Russian men who raped them!"

Herzl tried to choke back his emotions. Could they be seen on his face? He was sure they could not. "Europe's Jews will have a state of their own, or they will die," Herzl said simply. "To save them, I treat with men of power who have it in their hands to help my people achieve that goal, not with friends who can do nothing to help us. I meet with cabinet ministers and kings. Few of them care for Jews. Many believe the Children of Israel to be malodorous, criminal, and disgusting. It is of no concern to me. It is their hatred that provides the basis for dialogue. I wish to take the Jews out of Europe and they wish to be rid of them. I need the Ottomans to agree to Jewish settlement and autonomy, which they are reluctant to give, but which the czar, through appropriate pressure, might make it worthwhile for them to consider. The czar is worried about his Jews because they people the forces that oppose his regime and killed his father. The czar needs credit, and the Jews have bankers who can provide it. The czar needs allies and has suddenly realized that in the modern age, Western democracies will not want to be aligned with a bigoted autocracy. The Jews can offer good press if their interests are provided for. Under the circumstances, neither I nor His Excellency should be checking to see if the man sitting opposite him has horns."

Plehve, whose eyes had grown noticeably larger as he listened to Herzl's speech, now chuckled.

"Herr Herzl," he said, "you are a man after my own heart. The Devil is ready to bargain."

Dirty Jokes

The second hand on the old clock on the counter inside the café jerked at least five times before the men outside began to laugh. At first it was just Nissim, whose trinket shop was just up the hill on Strauss Street, on the border of Mea Shearim. He guffawed as if he didn't want to, as if guffawing were the last thing he should be doing at this moment, when they were about to set out for a battle in which many of them were sure to die. But he couldn't help himself, and when Shlomo joined in with a real belly laugh, coming straight from his very prominent belly, Nissim felt free to enjoy himself. Then Meir joined in, his thumbs pressing against the straps of the threadbare British para's pigeon vest he'd found somewhere to carry his ammo in. Arthur, the lost American with the mustache, banged his rifle against outside of the Ta'amon's display window so hard that Feibel looked up from his newspaper, wiped his hands on his apron, and shuffled out to yell at them.

When the laughter died down and Feibel had gone back to spreading out used teabags to dry, Nissim ventured to ask Pini whether any of it was actually true. Pini shot him a condescending glance and Nissim mumbled, "Well, the stories you hear about Paris!"

Shlomo started laughing again. He shook his head and chuckled. "That's real talent. It takes real talent to tell one of those jokes well. I mean, I can just picture them, the babushka and the rabbi and the convent girl! Where'd you learn to tell a joke that way?"

Pini shrugged and set his Bren on the ground. A ray of sunlight coming from behind the café bounced off a store window across King George Street and lit up the large bald spot on the top of his head. He rolled up the sleeves of his khaki shirt, revealing the squad's only real set of biceps as well as the number tattooed on his forearm. It had been cool just an hour ago on that May morning, when Richie woke them and told them that their People's Reserve Guard platoon, made up of unfit, middle-aged, and barely trained men, was going into action. An Egyptian battalion, fresh from victories in the south, had besieged Kibbutz Ramat Rachel, on the city's southern edge, and if Ramat Rachel fell, so would Arnona and Talpiot and then the enemy would march straight into the heart of West Jerusalem.

Until the joke, Pini had barely said anything since they'd been called up a few days before, after Ben-Gurion declared the establishment of a Jewish state in Palestine. Arthur, who'd done guard duty with him the first night in the pillbox on Gaza Road, later said something, in barely comprehensible Hebrew, about Pini having fought in Spain. Meir whispered, one morning when Pini was shaving in the far corner of the room where they were bivouacked, that Pini was the son of a bigwig at the Jewish Agency. Did you see the number? Doesn't he look too healthy and full of himself for a man who was there? There were stories about what he'd done in the camps. But then Pini had come back, clean-shaven and much better-looking than the rest of them, and Meir clammed up.

Again Shlomo asked: "Where'd you learn to tell a joke that way?"

Pini looked him straight in the eye. "Auschwitz," he said.

The men fell silent. They avoided his glance. Except for Meir, who looked straight back.

"At Buchenwald," Meir said evenly, "we were too hungry to tell jokes."

Pini considered Meir. "You were at Buchenwald?"

"Why? Is the face familiar?"

Pini shook his head.

"Buchenwald too?" Arthur shifted uncomfortably.

"After Auschwitz." Pini pursed his lips. "And the death march."

"I saw you get beat up by some *shkotzem*," Meir said. And to the others: "He deserved it."

Pini walked over to the curb, spat into the street, looked up and down to see if the bus they were waiting for was approaching. He walked back to face them.

"He was brought up for trial in a people's court," Meir explained. "He was a kapo there, in Auschwitz. Lackey of the big Polish thug who ran one of the barracks blocks. While other Jews starved, he ate well. They slaved and he whipped them. If they disobeyed him, he killed them with his bare hands."

The men froze in place. Nissim looked at Pini and shook his head.

"Must have been someone else," Nissim said. "They wouldn't have let him into the country, wouldn't have given him a gun if that was true."

"Helps when your father knows the old man," Meir said. "When you're a crown prince."

"Oh, lay off," Shlomo said, lighting a cigarette and coughing. "Let him tell another joke. Let me go out with a laugh. And a hard-on."

"Have you heard the one about Goering and the Valkyries?" Pini told it, acting out how the corpulent Luftwaffe chief leapt onto the stage at the Berlin opera house and tried to insert his member into the mouths of the Wagnerian altos. Shlomo doubled over and Nissim nearly turned blue before he could get some air in. Arthur couldn't possibly have gotten it but he laughed, too, and even Meir couldn't keep from smiling. But he didn't let go.

"This joker," he told his fellows, "was a kapo. Worked for the Germans to save his skin and that of his fellow Communists. Yes, he's a Communist. Still are, right, Pini?"

Pini shrugged. "For what it's worth, now."

"Hated the Jews, especially yeshiva boys and rabbis. Made sure they got sent straight to the furnaces."

Nothing moved in Pini's face.

"Pini sucked up to the Pole. To keep his position, he beat up Jews when he knew the Pole was watching, made them stand out in the cold for hours, sent men so sick they could barely walk out to hard labor. All to show he was more Nazi than the Nazis. That's how he survived." Meir stroked his gun. "I've got half a mind to put a bullet in him if the Arabs don't do it first."

"What difference does it make now?" Shlomo mumbled. "I'll probably never see my wife and girls again. Let me at least have some fun."

Pini told the one about the innocent French farm girl and Marshal Petain's silk diaper fetish.

Shlomo sank to the ground and beat it with his fist. "You're killing me! Where *did* you learn to tell a joke like that?"

As they wiped their tears away, Nissim looked as if he wanted to say something, then stopped. He finally blurted out: "Is any of it true?"

"I have a story about that," Pini said.

"Wait," Shlomo gasped. "Let me recover first."

Pini didn't wait. "It's night. Hundreds of skeletal men shivering six-seven on a shelf in an unheated shack in the Polish winter. In a room off to the side sits the block chief, a man who sent a score of men to their graves even before the Nazis arrived. Killing for him is like sex for us—he's got to get it every night. He keeps order by making a public example every night. Grabs a *zhid* and strangles him barehanded, douses a Slovak in water and sends him outside to freeze to death. Anyone who objects, who gets on his nerves, gets put on the list of the next morning's shipment to the gas chambers."

Arthur looked at him wide-eyed.

"That's what it looks like when I get there with a bunch of my Communist friends. Yeah, I'm a Communist. And you know what that means? When I see death standing in front of me, I don't pray and I don't give up. I'm not scared because I know I'm a cog in the machine of history, that my life means nothing except insofar as I let history use me to bring about the proletariat's ultimate victory over fascism. I'm a tool and I look around to see what my job is."

A rickety bus turned up King George from Jaffa Street and began rattling its way to receive them.

"And I see that the Pole gets enough food to be able to be horny. So I tell him that I lived in Paris and can tell him some real stories. Turns out that he likes them to be funny."

Richie waved at the bus. The men picked up their gear.

"So each night, once everyone's inside, I tell him a dirty joke. Long, as raunchy as I can make it. He goes into conniptions. I start another story and then promise to finish it the next evening. And you know what? A lot less people got killed."

"So all you did was tell jokes!" Meir spat. "That's not what they said at the trial."

Pini shrugged. "To tell the joke you have to have credibility. To have credibility you have to keep order. To keep order you have to beat some people up." He hoisted his Bren and boarded the bus.

On the way to battle, he told them about the one about the old whore and the seminarian, which had been a special favorite of the Pole's. The bus took them south, and as it climbed the hill toward Ramat Rachel, the Egyptians opened fire. A bullet took out Arthur. The rest of them scrambled out. Shrapnel hit Richie and made a hole in his belly. No one knew what to do. Pini crawled up behind a boulder and, as best he could from his inferior position, he tried to cover for his comrades by firing his machine gun in the direction of the enemy. It jammed. He looked around him and saw no one. He raised himself up on his hands to see if anyone else was firing and an Egyptian bullet pierced his neck.

Meir refused to go to the funeral, but Nissim and Shlomo went. After the brief ceremony, Pini's father approached them.

"Could you tell me," the distraught man asked them, "what his last words were?"

The two men looked at each other.

Nissim cleared his throat. "He told us how he saved the lives of Jews in Auschwitz," he said.

Shlomo began to laugh, uncontrollably, crumpling to the ground.

Stunned, the old man shook his head and walked back to rejoin his wife.

"I'm sorry, I'm sorry," Shlomo said, and Nissim could not tell now whether he was laughing or crying. "Pini was such a scream."

Hagar

Had she better breeding and fresher food, I might have called her a tortoiseshell. But she was an undernourished, neglected garbage-bin cat, a member of the local feral tribe that lives off the huge green dumpster in front of our thirty-eight-unit apartment building in Jerusalem. She caught my eye one morning when I descended to the office I've made out of our basement storeroom. She was curled up in the crib on wheels that we keep at the bottom of the stairwell. My wife, Ilana, runs a small preschool in our fourth-floor walkup, and the contraption is what the toddlers hold on to when she takes them out to the park. The cat gave me a mean look, scrambled out of the crib, and was gone.

At the bottom of the stairwell, with its bars and its sheeted mattress, the crib-on-wheels probably felt soft, dark, reasonably warm, and protected. I kept a cat when I was a kid, so I knew that pregnant cats seek out cozy places when placental hormones get into their bloodstreams. I made it clear to the faux-tortoiseshell street queen that she was unwelcome, and then made her birthing room uncomfortable by rumpling up a piece of plastic sheeting and placing it inside.

Few cats in Jerusalem are pets, but the feral cat population is huge. Dumpsters and garbage bins are located on the street and never close properly. Each one becomes the property of a feline community. The cats generally avoid human contact, but there's a long-established symbiosis. The human population produces refuse for the cats and the cats return the favor by hunting down any rats brave enough to compete for scavenging rights. At the time, our tribe—I liked to track its changing membership and pecking order—consisted of six or seven cats, led by a muscular, gray alpha male with white paws and a scar on his nose.

He wasn't doing much to help his pregnant concubine, certainly not getting her the prime pickings from the dumpster. She was scrawny and had the desperate, sideways gaze that I sometimes see among the mentally-ill indigents who live in the dilapidated housing project just up the street. Still, her choice of the crib-on-wheels certainly showed a kind of inspiration that no other pregnant cat had ever displayed before. I don't know where the dumpster's other expectant mothers went to whelp. Presumably they found crawl-spaces or crevices of some sort or another. But it was March, and this cat was looking for something dry and warm. In my mind, I began calling her Hagar, after the maidservant Abraham sent off to the desert, nearly killing her and their son.

Our building has four entrances, each leading into a stairwell that serves between seven and a dozen apartments. In our entrance, the neighbors were in the habit of leaving the outside door open. An ancient great-grandfather who had lived for years in the apartment closest to the entrance had complained about the noise of the door opening and closing, so it was kept open, and when he passed on, the habit remained. So the stairwell was generally accessible to Hagar. Over the next three or four weeks I frequently ran into her prowling the stairs, especially when it was raining or windy. She'd eye me suspiciously, standing her ground if I pretended not to see her. But the movement of my arm or a direct look in the eye sent her running outside.

About a month later, I returned from synagogue one Saturday morning and found a mess on my doorstep. Ilana keeps a large cardboard box on the landing, filled with old juice containers, plastic cosmetic jars, and yoghurt cups. Every so often she brings it inside and the preschool kids have a ball for an hour emptying the box, making up games with the discards, and putting them all back again. The box had been knocked down, its contents dispersed. I started tossing the discards back in the box when I noticed Hagar sprawled inside, barely conscious, with five still-bloody newborn kittens at her teats.

The birth must have occurred within the previous half hour; Ilana said she'd heard noises outside the door just a short time before. My initial instinct was to bring the box inside, but Ilana objected. She also pointed out that we couldn't possibly leave the cat family on our doorstep. It would hardly be sanitary, or even safe, to have an untamed feral cat mother protecting her kittens against the curious two-year-olds who came to our house five mornings a week.

I felt awful—Hagar was ugly and mean, but I admired her determination. Nevertheless, I gingerly picked up the box and started carrying it down the stairs. I had in mind a spot around back, a small, secluded alcove under a first-floor porch. Halfway down, Hagar woke up, stared at me in alarm, and leaped out of the box—sending two of the kittens flying onto the floor. I picked them up, but by the time I reached the entrance I couldn't see the mother. I was afraid if I took the box around back she'd never find them. So I put it in the garden near the door. Some of the neighbor kids caught sight of me and wanted to see the kittens, but I explained the situation and told them to keep their distance until the mother returned.

An hour later the kittens were gone, and I was uneasy. Maybe they'd been nabbed by ravens or by other cats?

Hagar disappeared for a day. I found her on Monday morning. Not in the crib-on-wheels, but right next to it. She'd taken over an old, dilapidated stroller that had been sitting under the stairs for many months, apparently without an owner. She was curled up in its tiny seat with two of the kittens. One was carrot-colored. The other was gray with white paws.

She didn't leave the kittens for a moment. Her body, wiry to begin with, grew emaciated. I couldn't imagine how she could produce milk without drinking. And so, on Wednesday morning, I put a saucer of milk on the floor near the stroller, but as far as I could tell she didn't touch it. I brought a piece of leftover turkey breast and placed it next to her in the stroller. She devoured it in three bites, gave me a dirty look, and stayed put. The stroller was beginning to stink and the neighbors were complaining. She wasn't going to be able to raise her kittens under the stairs.

On Friday morning, I found the kittens alone. Half an hour later, I saw her prowling outside, but she soon returned to the stroller. In the afternoon she left them again, and I took the stroller out and placed it next to the dumpster. I waited until I saw Hagar heading back to the entrance and followed her. She paid no attention to me as she trotted down the stairs and made the turn. She froze in her tracks when she encountered the empty space where the stroller once had been. She looked at me in alarm and meowed—the saddest, most desperate meow I'd ever heard. I walked slowly up the stairs and outside and she followed. But she wouldn't follow me far from the doorway. So I went and got the kittens and let her see and hear them, and then walked with them slowly back to the stroller.

My cruelty had reason behind it. The spot next to the dumpster was so unsuitable for raising kittens, I figured, that she'd immediately have to move them somewhere safe, and having been twice ejected from our entrance, she wouldn't risk taking them back there.

But the kittens remained in the stroller for the rest of that day and the next, their mewing growing steadily weaker. Sunday they, and the stroller, were gone.

During the months that followed, Hagar continued to prowl the grounds, often in the shadow of her alpha male. In early April, one of my downstairs neighbors went down to his storeroom to get a suitcase and found Hagar inside, with a new litter of kittens, perhaps a week or two old. She'd clawed a hole in the storeroom's window screen to get in. I helped him lift the suitcase up gently and place it in the garden. Soon the cats disappeared.

A couple months later, I notice that a new population of cats has taken over our dumpster. Hagar and her slipshod consort are gone, as is the rest of their tribe. One of the new cats, a sleek feline with an orange coat, begins prowling our stairwell. Is he Hagar's son? He looks well-fed and strong, and holds his ground almost until I touch him. I fear that he knows who I am.

Bananas

Yes, that's my seat, but don't worry about it, I'll just squeeze past, I've gained some weight and the belly doesn't squeeze like it used to, I'll sit over there next to you. No, really, it's fine. Yes, that's my name on the seat, but how could you know, you're a stranger, and who would bother to tell you because I hardly ever show up. Anyway, I built this synagogue, with some help from my brothers and sisters, so really all the seats are mine. Do I smell bananas or is it just my imagination?

That young rabbi gets on my nerves. See the way he parades behind the Torah scroll, looks just like Eli Yishai from the Shas party. I think at the yeshivot they bring in plastic surgeons and acting coaches to make them all look that way. Same short-trimmed beard, same beanpole physique, same clothes, same words coming out of their mouths. You think it's not polite for me to talk to you while everyone's blowing kisses at the holy scroll? Don't let it bother you. Like I said, I built this place and I can do whatever I want.

You know why I'm here? To say kaddish for my father. Died twenty-seven years ago today. And not a day too soon, believe me. He was a domineering bastard. You know the kind, from the old generation, no education, no knowledge of the world, no interests beyond telling his wife and kids what to do every day of their lives and every minute of their days. Each year I tell myself, enough, I won't go this year, but each year I wake up in a sweat on the day he died. He's been dead for nearly three decades but somewhere in my soul there's something that's sure that he'll give me a whack if I don't get out of bed and drive all the way from Shoham to Divrei Emet synagogue in Holon.

See that silver yad that the rabbi's holding up to point to the start of this week's portion in the Torah scroll? I donated that to the synagogue when my oldest daughter went to first grade. Pretty much everything here was paid for by my family. Those gaudy flickering orange memorial lamps that light up in sequence so that it looks like the Olympic torch being carried by a sprinter running up the Leaning Tower of Pisa? My brother-in-law donated those so that the souls of his uncle and aunt, killed in a horrible car accident five years ago, will go straight to heaven, as noted in large letters on each. And that impressive chandelier hanging from the ceiling over the bima, made of maybe ten thousand pieces of tear-shaped cut glass? Me and my brothers bought that for the synagogue in memory of our mother, a saint who had a very hard life, plagued by illness and fatigue, as inscribed on that large plaque hanging down in the center.

Where are you from? Jerusalem? Here visiting family? Where? Through that parking lot and up the stairs? I don't know them. Well, what do you expect, the neighborhood's changed since I was a kid here. This whole area was a refugee camp, hundreds and hundreds of families from Morocco, Tunisia, Iraq.

Okay, I'll whisper. The people have to hear the rabbi's sermon. He says the same thing every time I'm here. I'd rather be at the beach. What's the Torah portion this week? Balak? Yeah, it's always Balak.

We built the synagogue on the site of Abba's vegetable stand. See the street here, it wasn't paved back in the fifties. When the refugees got off the planes or boats they were bused here and left to make it on their own. Each family grabbed whatever empty space they could find. See that row of houses over there? That's where we lived.

I remember the story, I don't need to be told like a nursery school child. Balak, the king of Moab. Scared stiff of the Children of Israel swarming in the plain below his mountain kingdom. Calls in a famous sorcerer, Bil'am, from a distant land to curse them. Offers him a lot of money. Bil'am doesn't want to, but it's a lot of money. He's got a family, owes money to the magic store or whatever. So he goes.

We left Baghdad in '51. No, I didn't come with them. I was the oldest, I was already almost sixteen. I was in the French high school, star student, and my math teacher, a Jesuit from Marseilles, used some connections and arranged a ticket for me to Milan. He said that I could finish high school there and that if I served in the Italian army I could get a university scholarship. So they all came here and I went to Italy. Served in the signal corps and then did a civil engineering degree. I had a job offer, could have stayed there and by now I'd be retired in a villa in Tuscany, but no, Abba insisted that I come home. He needed me in the store. I'm an engineer, I wrote to him. First you sell cucumbers and get your brothers and sisters through school, then you can go be an engineer, he wrote. I don't know why I did it, but I bought a ticket and I came.

And I got off the bus, right over there, see through that window, there behind us, in my white suit, carrying my fine leather suitcase, and I stepped straight into a puddle brown with mud and donkey turds. The stench wallops me, latrine mixed with rotten tomatoes and unwashed human skin. And what do I see, a jumble of tents, shacks, lean-tos. I hear mothers screaming in exhaustion and children weeping and clementines, clementines, get your clementines, twenty agurot. And there's my Abba waiting for me, barely comes up to my shoulder, wearing a cast-off suit jacket with holes in the elbows and a pair of pants held up with a length of rope, and he puts his hand roughly on my arm and says, Ovad, look, here's our house and here's our store. And I look and what he says is a house is a box, literally a box, about the size of the foyer here, this is where my mother and father and four brothers and three sisters are living, and I stare and I say, Abba, where am I going to live, and he says, Don't worry, I thought it out, see those boards, we'll put them up on this side of the house and you'll have your own room. And he grabs me and pulls me down the street and through a field and we get here and points to four iron poles hammered into the ground with blankets hung between them and crates on top of crates of oranges and apples inside and he says, This is the store. And he starts shouting Clementines, clementines, twenty agurot! And I say Abba, I'm a civil engineer. And he puts his hand up and pinches my cheeks and brings my head down to his and says, Now you sell clementines.

So I sold clementines and in a month I looked like all the rest. Nearly forgot I'd ever been in Italy, ever gone to college.

I'll give Abba something, he never had a sick day in his life, not until the end. He wasn't a strong guy but if he had a fever or felt weak he just kept going, wouldn't even mention it, he'd just slow down a bit.

The last day? It was a steaming summer morning like this one. I'd left the store to take Albert and Hezi, my two youngest brothers, to the place where they got picked up for camp. Then I came back to the store and what do I see? The entire store is filled with huge stalks of yellow bananas with brown blotches, and outside the store on the street more and more stalks of bananas are piled up, you know, the thick stalks they cut right from the tree, with rows and rows of banana bunches on each one. There must have been a ton, maybe two tons of bananas, and they were giving off that sickly-sweet odor that means they're perfectly ripe. Which meant that on a hot summer day within two hours they'd be brown mush. I stopped in my tracks and stared. And what's Abba doing, he's crouched on the ground roasting an eggplant on a kerosene stove. He sees me staring at the bananas and he says, The jobber from Tenuva asked me to do a favor and take them off his hands. And I said, Abba, how are we going to sell so many bananas before they go rotten? And he said, You'll figure it out, and I said, I'll figure it out? And he said, I'm not feeling so well. When I was a kid and I felt this way, my grandmother would roast an eggplant and feed it to me. And he took the eggplant, charred and steaming, off the fire, blew on it, shook it, and then began to eat it, very slowly, peel and all. In the meantime, I hear all the hawkers on the street shouting Bananas! Ripe bananas sixty-five agurot! And I look and I see that each stall has one or two stalks of bananas. And we've got two tons.

Abba gets up and says, "I'm going home to rest for an hour or two."

I'm cursing him in my heart, telling myself to go back to the bus stop, get on the bus, look for a real job in Tel Aviv, and then I look at the bananas and I don't know what to do. I stare and stare and then I start dragging the stalks right into the middle of the street so that no one can get by and I put up a sign that says "Bananas 60 agurot." The other hawkers start screaming at me for undercutting the price and I scream back and they lower their price and I lower mine and before I know it the bananas are gone and the ten-kilo olive can that Abba kept his change in is filled to the top.

Abba hadn't come back yet so I tell my brother Tzion to watch the shop and I go home. Abba's sitting on the porch with the morning newspaper in his lap, staring into space. I go up to him. Abba! I say, but he keeps staring out into space. Abba, I sold the bananas. But he doesn't say a word. I bang the can down on the floor and coins go flying. Here's the money, I say. That's it, I've had enough, I'm leaving. No response. I pinch his cheeks with my fingers and force his head up so he's looking into my eyes and I say Abba, I sold the bananas. And then I see there's no life in his eyes. He's dead. Twenty-seven years ago today.

What? Yes, I left. I got a job as an engineer. Sent part of my salary home to my mother and brothers and sisters. Three years later I opened my own firm. Did very well. Paid for my brothers' and sisters' educations. We've all done well. Won't that rabbi ever stop talking?

Yeah, yeah, Bil'am tried three times to curse the Children of Israel, but each time the Holy One Blessed Be He put blessings in his mouth. Who doesn't know that story?

And I got my brothers and sisters together and we put up money and built this synagogue here, right on the spot where his stall stood, and I come here once a year to say kaddish in his memory. And you know what? All year I curse him, but on this day, one day a year, I miss him like hell.

My Big Fat Iraqi Hummus Joint

Ilana's got that look on her face.

"It's August," she says, "and all our friends are going to Corfu, Barcelona, and Antalya. But us? We're stuck here."

"If you wanted fancy European vacations, you shouldn't have married a freelance writer," I reply.

"J.K. Rowling is a freelance writer," she says, "and I bet she's not vacationing in Baghdad this summer."

"Who wants to go where everyone's going? Seasoned travelers know that the best spots are the ones no one's discovered yet. Besides, don't you want to reclaim your inheritance?"

"A burned-out store in the shuk? What good is that going to do me?"

"It may not be much now, but it'll be prime downtown property in a few years when Iraq is a flourishing Western-style democracy and a staunch ally of Israel."

There's that look again. "I can't believe you're serious."

"I've even found us a place to stay. Listen to this: The Babylon Hotel. On the banks of the Tigris, in Zuweia district, ten minutes from downtown. Two and a half stars."

"Nothing less than five."

"It had five until half of it was blown up by a car bomb last year," I say, pointing to the computer screen. "So there are special rates. We can just afford it."

"Is it recommended?" Ilana asks, peering over my shoulder.

"'Me and the boys make a trip every few months and always stay at the Babylon,'" I read out loud. "'No one bothers us as we carry a full complement of armaments including large caliber pistols, AK-4s, machine guns, grenade launchers, bazookas, and antitank missile launchers for our street use.'"

Ilana looks doubtful. "Doesn't that sound, well, a little risky?"

"Risk? We laugh at risk!" I remind her. "Remember at the height of the Second Intifada when no one was going anywhere and we refused to give in? We were practically the only guests at that hotel in Haifa."

"That was Zionism," she points out.

"So is this! We're off to return Jewish property to its rightful owners!" I bang the table for emphasis, and the picture of the Babylon Hotel on my computer screen wobbles as though if it might not stand much longer.

***

"Now I understand why Bush insisted on invading before summer," says Ilana. We're having a hard time pushing our way through the throng of shoppers. Our guidebook advised us that, in order to prevent heatstroke, we shouldn't go out in mid-day without an intravenous hookup. I'm holding Ilana's bag of saline solution and she's holding mine.

"According to your mother's directions, we turn left here," I say. "Hey, here it is!"

"That's a hummus joint," Ilana says.

"It is now," I say. Before the Farhud, the Iraqi anti-Jewish riots of 1941, this was her grandfather's tailor shop, where he made dress suits for Baghdad's wealthiest and most influential men.

A neatly-dressed young man with a thin moustache comes out to greet us. "May I show you to a table?" he asks.

"A table!" I cry. "You have the nerve to ask if we'd like *a* table?"

He looks uncomprehendingly at Ilana. Ilana gives me her look, but I ignore it.

"We'll take *all* the tables!" I shout. "They're ours!"

A slightly paunchy older man with a bushy moustache emerges from within. "Is something the matter?"

"If you don't behave yourself," Ilana hisses, "I'm going to drop your bag of saline and within minutes you will shrivel up into a human raisin."

"This is a matter of principle!" I cry. "We are returning Jewish property to its rightful owners! Namely us."

"Perhaps I can be of assistance," the older man says. He gently pushes us into a pair of shabby plywood chairs and motions to the young waiter, who returns with a pole for our IV bags and a large pitcher of iced lemonade. "I am Omar, and I am the owner."

"No, you're not. Well, I mean, you may be Omar," I say, "for all I know or care. But we're the owners. I'm Haim and this is my wife Ilana and her grandfather had a tailor shop here until anti-Semitic Arab rioters torched it in 1941. He was forced to flee to Jerusalem with his family and now we want it back."

Omar purses his lips. He breathes in deeply. He begins to turn red.

"He's going to blow up," Ilana whispers nervously.

"Okay," he says.

"Okay? Okay? All you can say is okay?" I place my face very close to his. "How dare you deny that this is our rightful inheritance?"

Ilana elbows me. "He said 'okay,'" she points out.

"But he doesn't mean it."

"Oh, I do," says Omar. He claps his hand, and the young waiter emerges with a manila envelope. Omar takes it from him and pulls out a sheaf of papers.

"Just sign here and here and here," Omar says politely. "There, thank you. It's yours," he says, and he walks away.

"Ha!" I say triumphantly. "And you doubted me." I look around at the small crowd that has gathered around us. I stand on my chair.

"Listen, all of you! No one pushes us Jews around, do you hear?"

The crowd, which consists of five Shiites, four Sunnis, a Nestorian Christian, three Mandeans (one lapsed), and two Kurds (one Yezdi, one Yârsân), applaud politely and then proceed to slaughter each other.

"Hey, Ahmed," I shout to the young waiter. "How about some hummus? We're hungry."

"My name's not Ahmed," he says. "It's Fred, and I'm an American here on a Fulbright."

Ilana, who is unsuccessfully trying to ignore the melee taking place right in front of us, wonders out loud: "Couldn't you find a less bloody way to earn your tuition money?"

Fred shrugs. "This is nothing. I tended bar in Fort Lauderdale last spring break. By the way," he says, turning to me. "You might want to read the fine print on those documents you just signed."

"What is fine print," I say, "when confronted with a very large truth?"

"Omar's not a local, you know." Fred smiles. "He's a Palestinian."

"Palestinian shmalistinian." I shrug. "I've turned the clock back. I've restored Jewish honor in Baghdad to where it was seventy years ago."

Fred laughs uncontrollably, and the members of the crowd, or more precisely those who are still alive, join in.

***

We're lugging our suitcases up the four flights of stairs to our Jerusalem apartment.

"Confess that you had fun," I say to Ilana.

"I'd confess to anything at this point," she says, panting. "Did I ever tell you that I murdered Haim Arlorsoroff?"

"The ancient river, the hospitality, the quaint local customs."

"I admit that I now have a much more vivid picture of what it was like to be in Egypt during the first plague."

My key doesn't fit in the lock. Neither does Ilana's. "Weird," I say.

I bang on the door.

It opens. I instinctively plant a kiss on the first available cheek, walk two steps in, then turn around.

"Omar?" I say.

"How's the hummus business?" he inquires.

"What the hell are you doing in my house?" I shout.

"It's my house," he says politely. "But you're very welcome."

"What do you mean, it's your house? Is this someone's idea of a post-Zionist prank?"

"You should have read those papers you signed," Ilana says. She's giving me the look again. I remove the manila envelope from my bag and pull out the papers. I raise them high in the air.

"Petty legalisms can't change the fact that this is a Jewish state," I declare. "It's the homeland of our people, where we have recreated our national and political life after thousands of years of exile."

"The establishment of state of Israel created an entirely new mode of Jewish existence. It negated the exile. Isn't that what you Zionists say?" Omar inquires.

"Precisely."

"So why, in Baghdad," he asks, "did you insist on returning to 1940?"

"To claim my rights."

"In 1940, you didn't have a state of Israel," he observes. "If we turn the clock back to 1940, then everyone has to go back to where their parents were then. I go back to Jerusalem, your lovely wife returns to Baghdad, and you," he says, pointing at me, but then hesitating, he looks at Ilana.

"Cleveland," she says. "He goes back to Cleveland."

"Ah, Cleveland!" Omar exults. "I have been there. Such hospitality. Such quaint local customs. And the river!"

"I would never live there," Ilana says. "Although, now that I've been to Baghdad, I might consider it for a vacation."

Is there a word for a deflated Zionist? No, of course not. I hand the papers back to Omar.

"Okay, okay. It's been nice making your acquaintance," I say, gritting my teeth. "And best of luck with the hummus joint. Now get the hell out."

"Actually," says Omar, "I kind of like it here. It's so different from everywhere else I've been. No river. No quaintness. No hospitality."

"Ha ha ha," I say.

But Omar is already at the door. He makes a courteous bow to Ilana and salutes me. "The point I wanted to make is that if you are going to take the country, you should at least let us have the Exile."

Rescue

My brother Levi says that if I weren't a woman he'd kill me. Just like the Arabs.

The reason he kills Arabs is that they are evil and kill us. He doesn't kill his sister because, he says, women think with their hearts and not their minds. Because they see only the here and now and not history. Because they trust too much.

So, I will spare you and let the Holy One, Blessed Be He, punish you, he says. That Arab could have killed you. Or worse. With you alone in the house. But now everyone in Meah She'arim knows. To them you're a whore. Soon you'll be called to testify in their courts and the whole Yishuv will learn of your shame. Perhaps that why your life has been spared, to receive that punishment.

As the summer of the year that the English call 1929 wanes, I ask you, My Rock and My Savior, is this so? More than seven weeks have passed since that Friday and Shabbat of slaughter and fear. So many of your people died. And I saved none of them. Instead, I rescued an Arab.

It was Friday, a bit after noon. I was alone, sitting on my high stool, plucking a chicken. A small one, as I would be alone on Shabbat. Shlomo was, is, in Europe, collecting funds for the kolel. You took Mother from me when I was sixteen. Father's mystical dreams soon took him to Safed, where he forgot about his children. Sarah married a Belgian businessman. She writes on occasion. You have not yet given me children. Levi, seventeen and wild, lives with me but learns long hours, so I am mostly alone. When the hours get too long, as they usually do, he runs off and plays soldier for the Zionists. He had already told me that he'd be on duty that Shabbat, probably at the Kotel, where the Arabs, may God take revenge on them, had thrown stones from the Temple Mount on our worshippers all week.

I did not know then, as I squinted in the dim light that came in through the small window behind me, that mobs of Arabs, stirred up by their preachers, had descended from their mosques intent on killing Your people. I did not know that they had fallen on the Gorji compound outside the Damascus Gate, slaughtering women and children, that they bludgeoned to death two brothers at Jaffa Gate. I was plucking a chicken and wiping sweat from my eyes and trying to keep my back straight and my spirits up. No one came to tell me. I heard rumbling in the distance, shouts, but I barely paid any attention. I suppose because people often shout in Meah She'arim. The heat clouded my eyes and made it hard to think. Whatever thoughts I had were elsewhere. I was crying softly and heard only myself.

I heard the sound of feet. Running, perhaps. My mind was elsewhere. The voices got louder. Someone banged on my door. I put down the chicken, wiped my hands on my apron, washed my hands, dried my eyes. I walked the few paces to the outside door, the one leading into the courtyard, and opened, not really thinking about who it might me. I suppose I assumed it was Rivka Levin from across the way, who bangs without bothering to knock first.

My eyes were dazzled by the sunlight. The shouts were louder now. Men were running out on the street, but in our courtyard all was quiet. The Levin girls were shelling peas. Some boys were tossing a ball, jeering at one who was not good at catching. A man stood before me, a small man, obviously an Arab, may they burn in hell, despite his carrot-colored hair. He was breathing hard. His shirt was stained with sweat. His mouth was wide open. He had gaps between his teeth. His eyes had dark circles around them, his nose was bright red, and his breath smelled very bad. His eyes bulged. I took a step back. I expected him to scream, but he didn't. I intended to slam the door, but then he whispered a word, over and over again. I couldn't quite make it out. Something like "*hilak.*" I don't know many of their words, their Arabic is very different from what Mother and Father spoke to us, but he kept saying it, "*hilak, hilak, hilak,*" gesticulating wildly and pointing to his chest.

He made me laugh.

And You know the amazing thing? He was not insulted. He held his pose, then looked behind him. Made a show of cocking his ear to listen. He sighed loudly and smiled broadly, as if to say he had not heard whatever he thought he might. Then he took a bow. Just like the hand organ man on King George Street does when you give him a grush.

Three Jews suddenly ran into the courtyard from the street, calling out to each other. Two had big sticks in their hand, one had a knife.

I grabbed my Arab, pulled him in, and slammed the door.

He stood there, a bit unsteady, by the table in the middle of the room. I poured him a glass of water from the pitcher I always keep there. He raised it, his hand trembling, but once he drank it down he seemed to recover. He looked around. The men outside were still shouting. A girl screamed and a boy cheered. It sounded like they were turning over washtubs. My Arab pointed to the bedroom and strode over. I followed him. Then he pointed at the cupboard. I opened it for him and threw out piles of Shlomo's shirts and my own underthings. He climbed in. I closed it behind him.

"Would you like some tea?" I asked him in Hebrew. "*Shai?*"

"*Shukran,*" he said, his voice muffled by the closet door.

So I went back to the kitchen and put the kettle on the primus. In the meantime, I perched on my stool and plucked feathers.

The outside door swung open and banged against the wall. I knew that sound. It was Levi. I picked up the naked chicken to singe it on the flame. He was panting.

"I need some water," he commanded.

I turned to look at him. His hair was every which way, his shirt half-open, his chest glistening. I approached the table and poured him a glass. He grabbed it and drank it down and held it out for more.

"We've put one where he belongs!" he exulted. Then he told me about what had happened at Jaffa Gate and at Damascus Gate. "But we won't let them murder Jews. For every Jew that dies, ten of them will fall. Another one got away and we're looking for him all over. I have to go. The boys are searching outside."

"I was going to make tea," I said.

"I don't have time."

"Stay a few minutes. You won't be here Shabbat. Give me just a few minutes." The kettle whistled.

Levi noticed the second glass on the table, drops of water still clinging to the side.

"Who's been here?"

"A friend," I said, pouring essence into three gold-trimmed tea glasses, and then adding boiling water. I added three spoonfuls of sugar to each.

"Which friend?"

"You don't know her," I said.

"I know all your friends," he insisted.

"Not this one." I smiled.

"You're pouring three glasses," he suddenly noticed.

I knew what would happen. How did I know? Perhaps it was like Father's mystical visions. But the bedroom door opened and my Arab walked out. He nodded at Levi and blushed. Levi eyed her suspiciously.

How did I know my Arab would change roles? But there he was, wearing a dress of mine, stuffed liberally at the belly and breasts with underwear. He'd wrapped his hair in a kerchief and tied it under his chin. It wouldn't have fooled any woman, but Levi, fired up with fighting spirit, did not look very closely. He never does.

My Arab smiled bashfully, reached out, took his tea glass, and shuffled back into the bedroom.

"She's folding the laundry for me," I said.

Levi slurped down his tea and handed me the glass.

"I have to go," he said. "Don't be frightened. We'll catch that Arab, and any other Arab who stalks Jewish women in our neighborhood!"

Levi's mind isn't the fastest, which is maybe why he skips out of his yeshiva so often. It took him a week to figure it out. In the meantime, the riots had been quelled and more than a hundred Jews had been massacred. Also, five Jews from our neighborhood had been arrested. They were charged with killing an Arab and attempting to kill Khamis al-Sayyed, a porter from the Old City. Al-Sayyed told the police that he'd run into a house in Meah She'arim and stayed there until late afternoon, after the mob had dispersed.

"It was you!" Levi shouted.

"Will you report me to the Haganah?" I asked.

"I'd kill you," he said, "if you weren't a woman."

Perhaps I am a bad woman, for I let a strange man into my home while I was alone. Into my bedroom. A man who was not even a Jew, God forbid. And I rescued an Arab, at the same time that his people were slaughtering mine. Oh, and I disobeyed my little brother.

A couple of hours after Levi left, the courtyard was in shadow and all had been quiet for some time. I went into the bedroom. My Arab was sitting on my bed. He had carefully folded up all the shirts and underwear and placed them back in the cupboard.

"I think you should go now," I said. "Will you be safe?"

He made a face and pointed to the dress and scarf he was still wearing.

"Of course," I said.

He opened the outside door just a slit, put his head out, looked around. Convinced all was quiet, he turned, and with a flourish gave me the same bow he'd given when he first came.

We both broke out laughing. He tiptoed out the door, through the courtyard, into the street.

The three reasons Levi will not kill me are these: Because women think with their hearts and not their minds. Because they see only the here and now and not history. Because they trust too much.

Let me add a fourth reason, my Creator. Of course, you know it already. You, after all, made me what I am: Some women laugh in the dark.

<h1 style="text-align:center">In Exile, at Home</h1>

After Sukkah 25b

The stranger is dressed in a threadbare sports jacket, which looks like it might have come from a second-hand shop, and a dusty black kipah. He strokes his short beard as he walks up and down the rows of graves at the Mt. Herzl military cemetery, stopping for a few beats at each to read the headstone. In the row in front of me he has to detour around t-shirt and shorts-clad twenty-somethings in a Birthright group, listening to a guide I can't hear. Finally he arrives at the last full row, where I am sitting. The lawn in front of the row waits for new tragedies.

He nods at me, hugging himself. I nod back. After a moment he speaks.

"It's cold here in Jerusalem."

I shrug. "Here we're used to the seasons starting to change the week before Rosh Hashanah. You must be from someplace warmer. Tel Aviv?"

"Tiberias. Also Sura."

I look at him quizzically. "You mean the one just west of the Euphrates?"

"That's where I studied." He holds out his hand. "Abba bar Zabda."

I shake it. "Haim," I say. "I can't place the name, though. I mean, I've studied a bit but I'm hardly a scholar."

"Yes." He sighs. "My wife wasn't pleased at all when she saw the final redaction. 'You're never home,' she griped, 'all day at the house of study, and then when they finally publish, they barely quote you.' I think it was because I have a knack for saying the wrong thing."

"Oh, wait a minute. Now I remember. You're the one with the vermin in the mikveh, the ritual purifying bath."

He smiles and quotes himself: "As long as a man holds vermin in his hand, he may bathe in all the waters of creation, but he will never be pure."

"That's a good one," I tell him. "I use it all the time."

"I appreciate that." He points at a vacant plastic stool. "May I?"

I motion for him to sit.

He nods at the grave. "Your son?"

A cool breeze blows through the cypresses, perfumed by the rosemary growing on the headstone. A pinwheel left by my oldest daughter twirls.

I nod. Then, after a minute: "I had some time between meetings, so I stopped by."

"That's good," he says. "It is a tradition to visit the graves of loved ones during the month of Elul."

"Yes, to steel yourself for another holiday without them," I reply.

"What's the hardest part of the holidays?"

I consider. "Maybe building the sukkah. He used to help me with that."

"Sukkot," he observes, "is the only holiday on which the Torah explicitly commands us to be happy."

"I do my best. But it's not the same."

"I might quote Ezekiel." He looks at me. "The prophet, I mean."

"Shoot."

"So he also lived by the river of Babylon. Centuries before I went to study there in Rav's academy. Ezekiel had a wife he loved dearly, and the Holy One, Blessed Be He, told him: 'Son of Man, behold, I am about to take the light of your eyes suddenly. But do not mourn or weep.' Put on your best clothes, spruce up your beard, and go about your business as if nothing happened. You, said God, will be a living symbol of the promise of redemption. Your people, living in exile, despair of redemption. I want them to look beyond their sorrow and loss toward My promise that I will restore them to their land. By going on with your life normally despite the blow you have suffered, you will show them that they, too, must live as best they can, looking to the future and not to the past."

I grimace. "Perhaps a prophet needs to be a public symbol. But I am not going to not mourn my son."

"Now you may wonder what this has to do with building a sukkah," Abba Bar Zabda says. He looks up and notices a clutch of Birthrighters listening in. "That's the holiday that begins on the fifteenth day of Tishrei, five days after Yom Kippur," he explains to them. "According to the Torah, Jews are commanded to leave their homes on this day and spend seven days living in a ramshackle hut, like the ones our ancestors lived in during their forty-year sojourn in the wilderness."

The American kids smile politely and whisper among themselves.

"Right, right," I say. "Get to the point."

"Now we might ask," he continues, clasping his hands together in his lap, "whether this law is incumbent on everybody, or whether in some cases one might be exempt. For example, is a mourner required to spend seven days in a sukkah if the holiday coincides with his seven days of mourning? And must a bridegroom spend seven days in a sukkah if it coincides with his seven days of rejoicing with his bride following his wedding?"

"You have a thing about sevens?" asks a blond Birthrighter with a Texas accent.

"Not me. The Creator." Abba Bar Zabda thinks a moment. "That's a good question, though. Why seven? Why not eight, or six? Is it just random, or is there a reason?"

The boy looks around at his companions and laughs. "I didn't mean for you to take it so seriously!"

"You mean," I suggest, "that a mourner is too wrapped up in his sorrow to rejoice in the sukkah."

"Right. Now, my teacher, Rav, who was the strict type, said that mourners must observe all the precepts in the Torah except for putting on tefillin." The rabbi looks up at the young people. "These things we strap onto our arms and heads when we pray. But then he also said that a person who suffers in the sukkah—I mean, if it's raining, or cold, or there's a bad smell—can eat and sleep in his home. What are we to make of this contradiction?"

"I guess if it's raining you can't do much about it," the Texan suggests.

"Very good," says bar Zabda.

"But that assumes a mourner is capable, by an act of will, of not suffering!" I object.

"Rav said that the mourner must compose his mind," the Tiberian says. "I'm not saying that I agree with him, I'm just reporting what he said. Now, what about the case of a bridegroom? He has an obligation to rejoice, so why shouldn't he do so in the sukkah?"

"Depends how big the sukkah is," says the Texan. "How big can it be? Can you fit a whole wedding banquet in?"

"Maybe the party isn't what was worrying Rav," I suggest.

"Quite possibly," agrees bar Zabda. "Certainly other scholars thought so. Abaye, for example, thought it was an issue of privacy, whereas Rabbah was worried about the bridegroom's discomfort."

"Privacy? At a wedding?" asks the Texan.

"At a traditional Jewish wedding," the Tiberian explains patiently, "the groom and bride retire, immediately following the ceremony, to a private room. I realize this may seem quaint today, but in my day this would be the first time they were ever alone together. And the expectation is that they would—and should—take advantage of the opportunity to consummate their love."

The Texan guffaws. "While everyone else is partying?"

"Abaye was concerned that the groom might need to step outside," bar Zabda expounds. "You know, he's nervous and his bladder might act up. And a sukkah is open and often built on a street or in a courtyard. Some other man could slip inside and compromise the bride."

"Not if she doesn't want to be compromised," says the Texan.

"The appearance of impropriety is no less problematic than impropriety itself," bar Zabda reminds him.

I consider. "Rabbah," I say, "must have been concerned that the nervous bridegroom might have trouble performing if he was worried that someone could walk in on them any time. Odd, however, that he doesn't consider how the bride might be feeling."

Bar Zabda shrugs. "I admit, back in the third century, we all had trouble seeing things from a woman's point of view. But certainly the bride would not find the sukkah a congenial place to be alone with her husband."

"So what's the conclusion?" I ask. The other Birthrighters have drifted off by now, but the Texan is still standing by us, listening.

"That the problem of privacy is not sufficient to cancel the obligation for the groom to observe the precept of sitting in the sukkah, but the problem of discomfort is."

"So, in short," I say, "a mourner is expected to collect himself and rejoice in the sukkah, while a bridegroom, who is rejoicing anyway, is given a break. Sounds counterintuitive to me."

"All mixed up," the Texan echoes.

"Let's go back to God's commandment to Ezekiel," bar Zabda suggests. "There, mourning is equated with exile. Ezekiel is commanded not to mourn his wife's death publicly, not to observe the rituals that make him look to others like a mourner. This is meant to be an example to the Jews in Babylonia, who are to live their lives and go about their business as if they had not been forcibly deported from their homeland."

I consider a minute. "A sukkah, too, is a form of exile. You're forced to leave your house and live in a rickety structure exposed to the elements."

"Yet in the sukkah we rejoice," bar Zabda says, encouraging me. He looks up at the Texan. "Maybe you can take that a little further?"

The boy ponders. "I'm not sure, but maybe—the bridegroom is moving in the opposite direction, leaving the exile of being alone in the world? He's actually going into his permanent home?"

"Not that I always understand the record of my respected colleagues' discussions," says bar Zabda. "The Talmud was not edited according to modern standards. But I think you are getting at something."

"A bride and groom do not need to be commanded to rejoice," I propose. "A mourner needs the commandment. Otherwise he will stay forever in exile and never be open to redemption."

The Texan looks around for his friends. "Sorry, I gotta go."

Bar Zabda holds up his hand, his thumb touching the tip of his forefinger. "We're almost done. They'll wait for you."

I glance at my son's grave. "It's not going to be easy. Isn't rejoicing when you've lost a child like dipping in a mikveh with vermin in your hand? You can never get clean?"

"I would say that, in this case, you need to hold fast and immerse yourself anyway," bar Zabda says.

"Wow," the Texan says. Bar Zabda nods at him, and goes off to seek his group. But he looks back once, then twice, on his way.

We listen again to the breeze.

"Ok, I'll do my best."

"Glad I could be of help." bar Zabda gets up. "I should get going or I will miss my bus home. Have a good year, the best it can be."

PART II: PERFECTLY NATURAL

Miss Violet's Piano

"It's the piano." Karin shivered. The music had woken her from an unremembered nightmare. "Someone is playing the piano."

Orr one-eyed her from under his pillow. His muffled voice sounded like it was reaching her from a cave below the floor.

"Call the police."

"My piano," Karin said. "Someone is playing my piano." She raised herself on her elbows, felt a creak in her lower back, and looked down at her research assistant.

Orr turned over on his side so that he could use both eyes. "That's impossible. There are two of us in the apartment. Of the two of us, only you know how to play the piano. And you are here. Ergo, no one is playing the piano."

An arpeggio sounded in the treble and was taken up by the bass.

"That is," Orr suggested, "unless a burglar, about to climb the basement window with his loot, was seized by an irresistible desire to play ... what is he playing?"

"Schumann. What do you care?" Karin snapped. Her cell phone vibrated.

She glared at him. "Aren't you going to do something?"

"It's your piano," Orr said, but he sat up and rubbed his eyes.

"You have scratch marks on your back," she noticed as the phone vibrated again. She reached out for it, glancing first at her nails.

Orr turned and looked at her. His black hair hung down below his shoulders and his chest was smooth. She swiped the green icon as he pulled on a pair of paisley boxers. Chords were jumping and the left hand seemed slightly out of sync with the right.

"We're going to check on it right now," she said into the phone, and then held it away from her as Mrs. Levi, the downstairs neighbor, had a fit.

"Maybe you should take a weapon," Karin said nervously as Orr shuffled to the door.

She pulled her knees up to her breasts and waited. The music had gotten quieter, not that it would make any difference to Mrs. Levi. Then it frantically crescendoed. She wouldn't be able to fall asleep afterward. Maybe she shouldn't even try, she considered. There were Roger's comments on her article that she had to go over. They'd arrived from California just as she was shutting down the computer but she was anxious to see what he thought and how much work she would have to do in response to his critique. Crystal-clear chords and unexpected dissonances sounded just as Orr returned. He stood in the doorway staring at her. He always did that. It bothered her.

"The piano," she said. "It's still playing."

"It is not," Orr said firmly.

"Stop acting like a four-year-old boy. Do you think I'm deaf?"

He started to climb into bed.

"Orr!" she reprimanded him.

He sighed. "Come," he said, extending his hand toward her.

She eyed him suspiciously. She grabbed her phone, pulled on her white robe, and followed Orr out.

The piano sounded clearly, alternating two themes, as they walked down the corridor from the bedroom. As they descended the narrow stairway that led to the music room, it was obvious that the music was coming from the old Steinway that had come with the house. The door was slightly ajar. Orr pushed it open and beckoned her in.

Silence. The room was still. The music had ceased. The lid was closed over the keys. Leaf-broken light from a nearly full moon filtered in through the high window that opened out onto the tiny, leafy Talbiya garden.

She felt for Orr's hand in the dark.

"That's not all," he whispered. "Look at this."

He pulled her out of the room and music again sounded, funny monkey-like rhythms and odd offbeat chords. He pulled her back in and the piano fell silent once again.

"Pretty weird," he whispered. It sounded like he was enjoying himself.

"I don't understand," she said.

"Now get this," he said, pulling her out. The music resumed. They stood in the corridor and he pulled the door slightly open. "Just look in, but don't step across the doorway."

Karin peeked into a drawing room with a well-polished sideboard bearing decanters and goblets. A dozen portly men in suits, many with moustaches, were seated in red plush chairs before a grand piano being played by a dark young woman. Something sparkled on her neck. Her eyes were fixed on the keys as her hands danced over them, as if the keys were pulling her fingers down and catapulting them to their next destination. The phone vibrated in Karin's pocket and the ringtone sounded.

"That's where the music's from," Orr whispered.

Karin unpeeked and looked at him. He motioned her to repeek.

The woman's face was now lined and her lips pursed. She was perhaps a decade older, dressed in a white blouse and dark skirt. The room seemed somewhat larger, perhaps because it was so sparsely furnished, its white walls almost bare. Men in white shirts and khaki pants and women who were dressed much like the performer fanned themselves with paper programs. Still she saw only the keys.

Karin stepped into the room and reached out toward the woman at the piano. The music stopped, the people all disappeared, and moon rays again searched their way through the window. She put her hands on her face, turned toward Orr, who still stood in the doorway. He pulled her toward him and lifted her pinching fingers from her cheeks.

She grabbed his hand and began leading him toward the stairs. "Let's get back to bed so that I can wake up normally. I have a ton of work to do in the morning. I have to finish my article and send it out. The deadline is Friday."

He held his ground. "This is kind of cool," he said.

He was pulling the door open again. She reluctantly followed his gaze.

The same woman sat at the piano, but now there was a girl sitting next to her intently watching the performer's fingers fly. The bench had been reupholstered and a small writing desk stood behind the piano. A brown teddy bear lay on top of a folding bed lodged between the desk and the wall.

Karin stepped into the room. The music stopped, and the moonlight returned. A drumroll sounded at the door.

"I'll get it," Orr mumbled.

Karin walked slowly around the piano. Now that her own children were grown, she didn't even need to put guests in this room anymore. All she did was play the piano, nearly every day, for a half hour, or hour, or until Mrs. Levi called.

Orr returned with the red-faced, house-coated matron. Mrs. Levi glared at Karin, glared at Orr, looked back and forth between them, and then fixed her gaze on the piano.

"I know the sound," she declared. "It's ruining my life for the last sixty years."

Karin recalled the generous offers her parents had made to buy out Mrs. Levi's floor, which would have given them the entire Arab villa and its yard. But no offer was ever good enough for the Levis.

Mrs. Levi reached over and sounded a black key. "You know what is strange?" she asked. "It didn't sound like you. In sixty years, you learn the neighbors' piano playing just like you learn voices."

"Well, there you have it," Karin said in relief.

"You know who played that way?" Mrs. Levi said. "Your teacher, Miss Violet. The one who wore the cross on her breast. I could have sworn it was her."

Karin sat on the bench.

"Who's Miss Violet?" Orr asked.

"She still comes here," Mrs. Levi complained. "You know that just last week I heard a clatter in my Menashe's room in the middle of the night, like someone was putting pots away in a cupboard. I opened the door and I saw Miss Violet in an apron. She gave me an evil smile and then disappeared. And I remembered that Menashe's room was their kitchen, before they left. And it was *not* a dream."

"Who's Miss Violet?" Orr repeated.

"My piano teacher," Karin said faintly.

"She was one of the girls that used to live here, before the war," Mrs. Levi explained. "And they ran away and left everything here. So when Karin's parents were given the upstairs and I got the downstairs, the piano was still there. Then, after we got Jerusalem back, Miss Violet showed up and asked if she could play the piano. She loved that piano and her parents had never been able to afford anything so fine again. So she used to come in and give Karin lessons and then they'd let her play a bit. That was one of her favorite pieces, the one she was playing tonight."

"Well, it's quiet now," Orr noted. "We should really all get back to sleep."

"Yes, go back to bed," Karin said. "Don't worry, I'll keep an eye on the piano."

Mrs. Levi surveyed the two of them disapprovingly and shook her head. "I never know what to expect in this house," she said, making her way to the door.

"I think I should sleep here," Karin said. "Help me get a mattress out."

"I'll stay with you," Orr said, pulling out the two mattresses that were kept behind the sideboard. "I'd kind of like to meet Miss Violet."

"I doubt she'll come." Karin opened a cupboard and surveyed bed linens in the moonlight. "She was very shy, especially around young men."

Orr flopped the mattresses on the floor. He looked at her for a few seconds. "Ok," he said. "You'll tell me in the morning."

"It depends," she said, "on the music."

Against the Odds

"The harira didn't come out so great today," the waitress says. "If you want soup, I'd go for the sweet potato."

Instead of standing, the waitress pulls up a chair. The father and his grown daughter are the only customers in the restaurant, which looks like it's been flown in from somewhere in Oregon, with its small tables and back-breaking chairs ranged around a large central unfinished wood counter. It's squeezed between an empty Ethiopian bar and an empty high-end Middle-Eastern grill, a bit east of the shuk, between Jaffa and Agripas. The stabbings are keeping people home, so the waitress has time on her hands.

She looks Oregonish herself, slender, with straight hair and large round glasses, clearly ten or maybe even fifteen years older than the standard student waitress. She's a single mother of two girls, she tells the father and daughter, and has just returned to her job, a few weeks after her baby was born, because how is she supposed to live?

The daughter looks around. "Did they let you have a celebration here?"

The waitress's face brightens. "Yes! Just last night! It was the manager's present to me. Just something small. Family, a few friends. All presided over by my grandmother, the Frau Doktor Dora Berman, who didn't like the food at all. She sat very stiffly over there, on that high chair at the end of the counter, in a black dress, nibbling from dishes we brought her, making faces. Mama was beside herself."

"How's the vegan lasagna?" the father asks.

"Abba, she's telling us about her baby!"

"But she's our waitress," he points out. "And I'm hungry."

The daughter fires a glare, but a loving one, at her father. "You can wait." Then she turns back to the waitress. "Your mother and grandmother don't get along?"

The waitress shrugs. "It's complicated. Mama can be a pain. But the Frau Doktor is one of a kind. Do you know what she said when I brought the baby in?"

"Should I guess?"

"We had this little ceremony." She puts her pencil and pad down on the table. "We got everyone singing. I brought the baby in along with Hofit, she's my three-year-old, and the idea was that I would pass the baby on to Mama and Mama would pass her on to Frau Doktor Dora and the matriarch would read a poem I'd printed up for her and then announce the baby's name. I'd explained it all to her and she knew exactly what she was supposed to do. And don't tell me she forgot, she's frail but still sharp as a crochet needle."

She reaches over to the next table where, unnoticed, a bag lies. She draws yarn and a needle out of it. Two balls, pink and white. "It's a hat for the baby," the waitress explains. The father looks at the daughter. The daughter ignores him.

"So I brought in the baby and gave it to Mama, and Mama bore her carefully across the room. Then, just as she was about to place the baby on her mother's lap, the Frau Doktor looked around the room regally and said, very loudly, 'You know, if I'd had that abortion, this one wouldn't be here!' My grandmother said this as Mama, her only daughter, was presenting her with her newest great-granddaughter!

"Well, Mama grabbed the baby back and turned around and I saw tears on her cheeks. 'How could she ruin such a moment?' Mama hissed between her teeth. I was in shock, we were all in shock. Then Frau Doktor Dora put her hands to her face, her chest heaving, gasping for air."

The father points at the menu. "The coconut curry. Does that have milk in it?"

The daughter gives him a look.

"You can get it with milk or we can do it with coconut milk," the waitress says. "Well, of course the singing stopped and the whole place fell silent. And then Frau Doktor Dora removed her hands from her face, smoothed down her dress, looked around her, and began to lecture."

The waitress falls silent, her hands busy with her needles.

The father takes the waitress's pencil and jots on her pad. He pushes it over to his daughter. "*I thought the place was empty because people are scared to go out, but now I think it might be the service.*" The daughter pushes the pad back with her reply. "*Story now. Food later.*" Sighing, the father puts his menu on his lap.

"'It was in early 1944 that my period stopped,'" the waitress intones, changing her voice to her grandmother's scratchy alto. "'January went by, then February, then March. I worked part-time as a secretary in the Generali building, paid under the table and pinched by Advocate Wolfe. He liked to tell his clients that his secretary had a German law degree but that, unfortunately, German law had outlawed her from practicing German law, and she was lucky to be filing papers for him in the Land of Israel. Others like her were mopping floors.

"'It wasn't until April that I got up the nerve to tell Aryeh. We lived in a tiny room off Jaffa, not far from here, sharing a kitchen and bathroom with two other families. The rent cost more than my salary. Aryeh worked as a house painter—he hadn't been able to finish his engineering degree before we fled. But he'd fallen off a ladder and broken his leg, so he hadn't worked for two months. He was depressed and angry at the world. If you have the baby, he said, Wolfe will fire you.'"

The waitress holds up the cap. "What do you think?" she says in her normal voice.

The daughter reaches out to touch. "It's beautiful."

"So they asked around and got the name of a surgeon who had a one-room private clinic in Talpiot. And he said it would cost five Palestinian pounds, but they didn't have the money and had already borrowed from the only friends who could afford to help them. They asked him if they could pay him one pound a month, one for each month until the baby would have been born. He refused.

"A week later, my grandfather hobbled over to the Generali building. He slipped an envelope under the door of Advocate Wolfe's office, went up to the roof, and jumped off. Wolfe fired his overqualified secretary, and Mama was born a week before Rosh Hashanah.

"'Give me the baby,' the Frau Doktor commanded. Mama glanced at me and I nodded, and she laid the baby in my grandmother's lap. 'This baby owes her life to a stingy physician,' she announced. 'And her name in Israel will be ...' She looked down at the paper I'd given her. 'Tzofia. What kind of name is that?'"

"Great story," says the father. He rips off the page he and his daughter have scribbled on and nudges the pad hopefully in the waitress's direction. He also picks the menu off his lap. His daughter kicks him under the table. The waitress sighs. She looks out the window.

"You know, there was a stabbing right over there last night." She points with her chin.

"Awful," the daughter shudders.

Sticking her needles in the yarn, she puts the unfinished hat back in her bag and takes up her pad and pencil.

"I think I'll have the lasagna," the father says. "And maybe you can recommend a first course we can share?"

The daughter smiles. "I'll just have the sweet potato soup."

"I'll bring you half a bottle of white wine left over from the party," the waitress says. "On the house." She's about to head for the kitchen, but the daughter stops her.

"What happened then?"

The waitress shrugs. "There was this long moment of silence. Then all the sudden we heard shouts, then sirens. We all ran out to see what happened. Everyone except Frau Doktor, who remained on her throne. A terrorist stabbed a woman, did you hear? He was just a kid. No more than sixteen, seventeen, from the look of the body. A soldier shot him. The police came and an ambulance took him and the poor lady away. I read in the paper that she was the mother of two. When it was over, we all came back in. Then Hofit, my three-year-old, piped up and said 'Is her name really Tzofia?' And Frau Doktor gazed down on her and said: 'You don't believe me? That's what it says here!' And then someone shouted 'Mazal tov!' and then everyone started singing and we brought out the food."

"Bringing food sounds like a great idea," the father says.

"You probably think I have a pretty strange family."

The daughter nods in the direction of her father. "So do I."

The waitress laughs. "I'll probably be as bad as Frau Doktor if I make it into my eighties."

"She had a tough life," the daughter observes.

The waitress looks out the window, to the spot where the woman had been murdered and the teenage terrorist killed.

"It's like we're all alive just by chance." She shrugs. "Think of it. Against the odds. I'll go put in your order."

Sin Offering

After Baba Batra 10b

"Please confine yourself to discussing your own sister's anatomy," Yohanan said as he smeared iodine paste on the gash in Josh's shin. Yohanan was smiling despite himself because Josh had mispronounced the expletive, as he mispronounced most everything he said in Hebrew. Josh was lying back on his elbows on a scratchy slate-colored army blanket spread over the yellow grit of the Negev borderland. The medic used his whole slender arm, moving it from the shoulder, where others used only their wrists and hands. Josh grimaced and grabbed the grimy purple kipah off Yohanan's buzz-cut scalp. He kissed it, replaced it, and gave Yohanan the finger. The sun hung heavily over the plain to the east, behind a scrim of dust, as if it had barely risen this far and would go no further. Another blanket lay behind them, not smooth but lumpy. Something small underneath.

"Holier than thou," Josh muttered in English. Yohanan jerked his head and his kipah fell onto Josh's belly. So did his glasses. Josh handed the glasses back to Yohanan and put the kipah on his own head, trying it out for a moment before giving it back. Intently kneeling over Josh's leg like a penitent on a pilgrimage, Yohanan wound the gauze bandage. Josh picked up the tube of iodine to examine the expiration date. "It better be good stuff," he said. "That whore-daughter's mouth is probably full of animalcules. Rabies. AIDS. Hepatitises A through C. Ebola and plague."

"You're good to go," Yohanan said, rolling down the leg of Josh's fatigues and slapping him on the knee.

"Until the infection sets in," Josh said portentously. "I can't believe she bit me. Like a snake."

Sergeant Eliezer, the only one standing, eyed his friends as he swayed in prayer, running his left hand over his beard and then clasping it, before him, to his right.

"What do you expect from them, they're animals, those Sudanese," came the muffled voice of Modai. The stocky machine-gunner, lying flat on his back in the sand, had placed his hat over his face.

"And here I thought they were human beings like us," Yohanan said, packing his medical gear back into his vest.

Eliezer, stepping back from his prayer, sat down to join them, quickly unwinding his tefillin from his arm. "A human being is not what a person is," he said. "It's what a person does. King Solomon says: 'Tzedakah teromem goy; ve-hesed le-umim hatat.'"

Josh looked uncomfortable.

"Proverbs 14:34," Eliezer said.

Josh's fingers dashed over his iPhone and had the translation in hand in just a few seconds. "Righteousness exalts a nation; benevolence for a people is a sin," he read out, just as Gamliel strode over. Yohanan poked Modai and hissed, "Company commander!" Modai peeked out from under his hat and sat up.

"What was that?" the commander, Gamliel, asked.

"Tzedakah teromem goy; ve-hesed le-umim hatat," the sergeant said. The expression on his face differed from the others. It was defiant, almost hostile.

Gamliel ignored him. "Sit down, all of you. Give me the story." The soldiers formed in a semi-circle in front of him, holding their M16s between their knees or on their laps, avoiding the gaze of the sun.

"We received the sighting of the figures at 0435 hours," Eliezer said, jerking his head to indicate the radio set at Josh's side. "We rushed over to the site, at the coordinates given."

"We were there in a flash. I drove like a maniac," Modai crowed, but Gamliel shushed him.

"I want to hear Eliezer."

"About 300 meters from destination, behind a fold in the terrain, we halted the jeep and unloaded. Modai stayed with the jeep and the rest of us proceeded on foot. Approaching the fence, we heard a clicking sound. I signaled to the guys to get down. First light was just coming in, and I saw a cluster of Sudanese crowding around the fence. Four adult males, a teenage boy, and one woman. The woman, as tall as the men, was cutting a hole in the fence with a small pair of wire clippers. I was surprised at how much strength she had in her hands given how scrawny they all were. The four men were gathered around her, looking pretty helpless. She was wearing a kind of ragged smock and had something strapped on to her front, and I was worried that it was a bomb. We took cover, and I called out '*Waqf!*' But she didn't stop, she just kept cutting away at the fence."

Yohanan tossed a stone at some imaginary target. "Four adult men, a teenage boy, and a young woman carrying a ..."

"Blacks. From Sudan," Josh said excitedly. "Illegals."

"Eliezer." Gamliel said it firmly, jerking the rifle hanging from his right shoulder.

"I called out another warning in Arabic, according to orders," Eliezer continued. He chose his words carefully. "Then I signaled to Josh to warn them in English."

"Turn back!" Josh cried, quoting himself. "You have been spotted. You will not be allowed to cross the border."

"She just kept at it," Eliezer said.

"'Halt or we will shoot!'" Josh called out.

"I fired a warning shot."

"Pow!" That was Josh. Yohanan glared at him.

"The men looked up," Yohanan said quietly. "But the woman …"

Eliezer cut him off. "The woman slowly raised her head and looked me straight in the eye. She hung the cutter on the fence—the breach was big enough to step through by now—and put her hands on the bundle hanging in front of her. I ordered Yohanan and Josh to cock their rifles …"

"It was a baby!" Yohanan's eyes were intent on a pebble he was tossing in the air.

"'Hadal!'" Josh called out. "She shouted, 'Hold your fire! Hadal!' In English and then in Hebrew!" He looked around at the others.

Eliezer glared at Josh. "Then, in a single move, she pulled the baby out of the sling in front of her and tossed it at us."

"It was like slow motion in a movie," Yohanan said. "The baby sailing through the air."

"It was coming straight at me," Josh said. "I let go of my rifle and held out my hands, and, plop! There it was in my arms."

Gamliel looked confused. The shadows of his soldiers seemed to be growing longer, stretching to the west. "She tossed the baby? You caught it?"

"I was covering from the jeep. I saw it," Modai confirmed.

"'She cast the child under one of the bushes.'" Eliezer quoted the story of Hagar the slave-woman from Genesis. "Would a Jewish mother do such a thing? Abandon her child?"

"I think it was dead," Modai said. "It didn't move."

"Not so," Josh said. "Not then. I saw its eyes."

"'Righteousness exalts a nation; benevolence for a people is a sin,'" Eliezer reiterated.

Gamliel opened his mouth to say something, then closed it without having gotten a word out. After a few seconds, he asked: "What does that have to do with it? What nation, what people?"

"It's pretty obvious." Eliezer raised his voice, ready to dispute. "The first half of the verse refers to the people of Israel, who act in righteousness and are exalted by God. The second half refers to the gentile nations, who live lives of sin."

"Calm down. This is a military debriefing, not a yeshiva," Gamliel ordered. Eliezer was about to protest, but Yohanan gave him a warning look and he thought the better of it.

Yohanan stared at Eliezer and threw a larger rock into the distance. "It's righteous to send starving refugees to their deaths? You know the Egyptian army will kill them, if they don't die of hunger and thirst first."

"Did I do something wrong?" Josh pleaded, looking at his buddies, seeking reassurance. "Look," he said, "I feel awful. But we're a Jewish state, right? How will we be a Jewish state if half of Africa comes here? Are they our responsibility? Why don't the Egyptians give them shelter? Why are we always guilty?"

"Yeah," Modai piped up. "We're soldiers in the world's most moral army. When they get into our territory, look how we treat them. Give them food, tents to live in."

"Can't the whole proverb be about us, Eliezer?" Yohanan asked. "And about the others, too? We're Jews, not angels. Sometimes we do what's right. Sometimes we sin. So do other people. They do good deeds, don't they?"

"'Who is like your people Israel, a unique nation on earth,'" Eliezer shot back. "We are different. Even when the gentiles do good deeds, they do it for their own good, to enhance their wealth and power, and to oppress and kill us."

"Let's get back to the incident," Gamliel said. "Wait a minute, it was just the four of you there?"

They all looked around.

"Nehuniya!" Modai shouted. Then he explained to Gamliel what Gamliel already knew: "It takes him a long time to pray." At that moment, the missing soldier appeared, as jumbled in his dress as Eliezer was groomed, his beard scraggly compared to Eliezer's carefully trimmed one, his sidelocks swaying in the breeze. He kept his left hand almost permanently on the topknot of his filthy white knitted Nahman cap, moving it a centimeter this way and an inch that. He still had his tefillin on.

"Where were you during the incident?" Gamliel asked him, motioning for him to sit down beside the rest. Nehuniya remained standing, staring into the sun. After a moment he said: "Where was I?"

"It's a difficult question for him," Modai explained to the officer. "He never really knows."

"We should read it this way," Nehuniya suggested. "'Righteousness exalts a nation, it is benevolence, for *other* people it is a sin.' All the good words for us, guys." He giggled.

"Shut up and sit down!" Gamliel shouted. "This is a debriefing after a serious incident in which one of my soldiers was wounded. We are not holding a Talmudic disputation!" He pointed to Josh. "You had the baby in your hands."

Josh looked down at his hands and held them out in front of him. "Yes, like this."

"She stood there and pulled herself up and started making a speech," Eliezer said. "In Hebrew. 'I have lived among you,' she said. 'I came over this border, not far from this spot, before you built a fence. I lived among you in a slum in Tel Aviv for five months, scrubbing floors for a few shekels an hour under the table. But my parents remained in Sudan, my brothers, my cousins.' She looked at the men around her. 'The soldiers there would come to our village and rape and murder. I went back to get them. Not many were left when I arrived, and more died along the way. These are all who are left. You can shoot us now. You can send us back to die.'"

Yohanan rose to his feet. He slung his rifle over his shoulder and placed himself next to Gamliel. "She wept. 'I fell in love there. My lover was killed by the soldiers.'" Yohanan pulled a piece of gauze out of his pocket and wiped his eyes. "'This is my daughter. Give her a home.'"

The soldiers were silent.

"I went up to her," Josh said. "'You can't abandon your baby,' I said. 'You have to take care of her.' And I handed it back. Wasn't that the right thing to do?"

"She stood there," Nehuniya said. "She placed her right hand on the baby's forehead, and whispered something, looking skyward. Then she took the wire cutter off the fence."

"You were there?" Gamliel glared.

"I think I was," Nehuniya said. "Although I was thinking of something else."

"Suddenly, she fell to the ground," Eliezer said. "Right on top of the baby. I thought she had fainted."

"And she grabbed my leg and pushed my pants up and sunk her teeth into my shin," Josh said, grimacing. "Why did she do that?"

"Because you gave her baby back to her," Modai said sarcastically. "Why should she want her baby? Just a burden to her."

"Then she got up," Yohanan said. "She brushed herself off. She wiped the wire cutter, smearing a reddish stripe on her smock. Then she turned back, into Sinai, and trudged off slowly, painfully. The others followed. The baby remained there, by the breach in the fence."

"You're such a wimp," Eliezer sneered. "Maybe we should have taken the wire cutter from her and taken down the fence ourselves."

"Hatat," Yohanan said. "It doesn't really mean sin, Gamliel. It's a sacrifice."

Nehuniya nodded. "An offering on the altar in the Temple. To cleanse you of your sins," His voice sounded as if it came from far off.

"Righteousness exalts a nation; benevolence for a people is a sin offering," Yohanan said. "When we are charitable it exalts us, and when other nations are charitable, it purifies them of their sins. Can't you read it like that?"

"No," Eliezer said firmly.

Josh slowly rolled up the leg of his fatigues and gazed at the bandage.

"My blood ..." he said. His voice trailed off. He choked.

Gamliel looked behind him. Was the sun setting in the east? "Where's the baby?" he asked.

Yohanan jerked his head at the lump behind them. Josh rose to his feet, walked heavily to the blanket, and picked it up, together with the small body it covered. Shaking, he walked back and presented it to Gamliel, who stepped back and refused the offering.

"It's my sin," Josh said. "Or is it hers?

"When they get to the holy mountain," Yohanan said, sitting down again, searching for a rock to toss. "God will tell them. And who else to offer up on the altar."

Possession

"Look. It's a 'B,'" said Sally.

Sally was going to be fourteen on Tuesday and she was making cookies for her party along with her friend Ruthie. The coloring leaves of a fine Cleveland autumn afternoon were filtering the rays that came through the window over the sink. Sally's mom was hovering around, making sure the mess didn't get out of hand. The oven was already hot and the girls didn't always check to make sure the refrigerator door was properly closed. Sally had just missed getting an egg into the mixing bowl and was trying to push it with a sponge into the sink when she looked straight at her Mom and made her pronouncement.

"B," Sally pronounced, "is for Brad."

Ruthie blushed.

"Who's Brad?" Janice asked. She leaned over Sally to wipe egg yolk off a new white cabinet door. Even with one less person in the house, the kitchen was too small, she griped to herself. Why weren't the cabinets out of splattering distance?

"A new kid in our class," said Ruthie.

"Ruthie's madly in love with him. She's been praying day and night for him to call her."

The telephone rang.

"I'll get it," Janice said. She took two paces to the wall phone and, bringing the receiver on its long cord back to the counter, she spotted a couple of squiggles of egg yolk in a sea of clear albumen that indeed looked something like a B.

"Hello," she said, tugging at the cord.

"Mrs. Greenberg?" an adolescent voice squeaked.

"Yes, that's me," Janice confirmed.

"Um—may I speak to Sally?"

"Whom may I say is calling?"

"Brad."

"It's Brad," Janice said, holding the phone out to Sally. She winced as Sally wrapped her damp floury fingers around the receiver without wiping them first. Janice placed a hand lightly on Ruthie's shoulder. Ruthie was looking a little weak.

"Hi Brad," said Sally. She held out the phone so they could all hear.

"Um, Sally, I was wondering," said the squeaky voice. "Do you have Ruthie's telephone number?"

Ruthie wobbled and might have sunk to the floor if Janice hadn't been holding on to her.

"As a matter of fact," said Sally, "she's right here. Would you like to talk to her?"

"Hey—sure." Sally passed the phone over to Ruthie. Ruthie gave her an imploring look and Janice pushed up a chair, which Ruthie sank into as she gripped the phone to her ear. The conversation was short. Ruthie handed the phone back to Sally, Sally passed it on to Janice, and Janice placed the receiver back on the wall.

"We're going to do math homework together tonight," Ruthie swooned.

"See, B is for Brad," said Sally, pointing to the egg on the countertop. Janice looked again. The B was still there.

***

B is for Brad was followed later in the week by G is for Grandma, when Sally insisted on making scrambled eggs on Thursday morning even though she didn't have time to cook and eat them and get to school on time. After half-whisking white and yolk together she found a hazy yellow G in the bands of yellow in the bowl.

"But there's these dark dots next to the G and that means something bad is going to happen," Sally told Janice matter-of-factly. "But it's only three dots so it won't be so bad. If there were five dots I'd worry."

Janice saw the G and the three dark dots before Sally poured the eggs into the frying pan. At ten that morning, just after she arrived at her box-filled office at Temple Emmanuel, the phone rang. It was her sister calling from Memphis to tell her that their mother had fallen down a few stairs at the entrance to her apartment building. They were in the emergency room. She seemed to be fine except for an ugly bruise but they were doing an x-ray to make sure her hip wasn't broken. Mom was in good spirits and told Janice to stay home with Eric and Sally and stop the silly talk about flying all the way from Cleveland just to bother her.

"By the way," she said, "have you heard from Joel?"

"Not a word," Janice sighed. Joel, her husband, had simply disappeared from her life a month before. He left a note saying that he knew everything now, that he had never thought that this would happen to him, that he was devastated and never wanted to speak to her again. They would meet in court about the kids, whom she wasn't fit to raise. He sent Eric and Sally email messages that they did not show her. Janice had no idea where he'd gone.

"All I can say is that your Rabbi Weiss got what he deserved," Mom said for perhaps the seventy-fifth time. Rabbi Weiss, only forty-eight years old, had suffered a fatal heart attack just as he finished reading the confession on Yom Kippur. His congregants, who were standing dutifully and waiting for him to tell them what page to turn to, watched in astonishment as their rabbi emitted a loud groan and crumpled to the floor. His wife, Linda, and seventeen physicians and specialists of the highest caliber, one of whom was Joel, a pathologist, ran up to the bima but to no avail. Janice held her scream tight inside her. She and Rabbi Ezra Weiss had been lovers for half a year.

"And what do I deserve, Mom?" Janice asked.

"You're my daughter, so you deserve the best. I don't know how he managed to destroy you. You've always been such a wonderful wife and mother."

"Whatever I did, I did of my own volition," Janice said. "I've messed up my life, but Ezra was a fine and gentle man."

"I didn't raise you to have a volition," Mom said. "Have you found a job yet?"

"I'm still cleaning out my office."

"In my day, we wouldn't have had a woman as our temple's executive director, and if we'd had one we wouldn't have left her alone in the building with only the rabbi around. Two people can go crazy when they're alone in a large building."

"Yes, Mom," said Janice. "Call me as soon as the doctor reads the x-rays."

***

It hadn't really begun because she and Ezra were alone in the synagogue together. That facilitated the affair when it began, but the fact was that they'd often been the only ones in the building during the three years that Ezra served as rabbi, and nothing had happened. The reason the affair began, at least as far as Janice was concerned, was that her soul had split in two.

Her soul, when she first realized it was there in adolescence, was a faintly glowing blob that resided just below her breastbone. She never spoke of it to anyone, even to Joel, who had made the blob glow bright when they met.

But in the years after Sally was born the glow gradually faded and her soul became less illuminated and more blobby, until she felt that what she had inside her was a large amoeba. It seemed the right kind of soul for the routine of her life, heavy and squishy. With this kind of soul, one did one's job and performed one's duties and felt good about it. Things were okay and they remained more or less okay for a long time.

About a year ago, though, the amoeba split in two, as amoebas do, and there were two of them. One half remained a blob. The other half began to glow whenever she saw Ezra Weiss. She'd admired Rabbi Weiss ever since the synagogue hired him. He was soft-spoken, considerate, intelligent. He seemed to have a special knack for sensing when a dispute on the board was about to develop into one of those personal feuds that are the bane of all congregations. By simply giving his full attention to each side as they spoke, nodding sympathetically, and then pointing out to the two that they in fact were in agreement on most of the really important points, he enabled them to put their differences in perspective and resolve them. It was watching him at one such moment, a particularly delicate one that he navigated masterfully, that Janice started thinking of him as a man.

One day, Ezra peeked into her office and the glowing blob transformed itself into a circle of light. Half an hour later, the circle of light belonged to Ezra. The blob belonged to Joel.

***

In the two weeks that followed, various eggs, beaten or simply broken into a little glass bowl or straight into the frying pan, showed Sally a C with a halo, meaning that the cat would get run over, which she did; and an E with a sort of patch of cloud to its upper right, which meant that Eric was smoking pot in his room, which he was. A J with a curlicue on top, according to Sally, meant that Dad's lawyer would call. She got this slightly wrong: it was a registered letter, not a phone call. And then there was a very distinct 89, which Sally said would be her grade on her geography exam, which is exactly what she received.

"What do you think it means?" Janice asked Sally at dinner the night after the geography grade was confirmed.

"It means she's a snitch," said a glowering Eric as he speared a chicken leg.

Sally shrugged. "I don't know. It's kind of fun."

"Can you do it whenever you want?" Janice wondered. She got up, took an egg out of the refrigerator, the egg bowl from the cupboard, and placed them before Sally. "Try."

Sally broke the egg into the bowl and mixed it up with her knife.

"Do you see anything?"

Sally looked closely. "No."

Eric leaned over. "It says that Sally's a snitch."

Janice looked and didn't see anything either.

"When you see something, how do you know what it means?" she asked her daughter.

"Rabbi Weiss tells me," Sally said.

"You rude, nasty little girl," Janice screamed, except she didn't scream, she kept it inside. What she really said, as she gripped the table tightly was: "What do you mean, Rabbi Weiss tells you?"

"He whispers in my ear," Sally explained.

"Are you nuts?" Eric demanded to know. "Rabbi Weiss is dead."

"I hear his voice in my ear," Sally said defensively. "You can't say that I don't."

"You don't."

"You're jealous."

"Sure, like I want to hear Rabbi Weiss whispering in my ear." He glanced at Janice and added: "Mom might."

"Eric!" Janice shouted, for real now.

***

After the dishes were done, Eric went out to play basketball, and Janice and Sally sat down to watch television. During a savings-and-loan commercial, Sally suddenly stiffened and turned to face her mother. Her eyebrows were raised painfully high and her cheeks tensed as if someone invisible were pulling her whole face back. Then Sally said: "I am in great pain." But it wasn't Sally's voice.

Janice wanted to scream. She tried to take her daughter's hands in hers, but Sally yanked them away.

"I am in great pain, Janice." The back door opened and Eric walked in, wearing a sweaty t-shirt and shorts and carrying a basketball. Janice gave him an imploring look. He walked over to Sally and stared at her.

"We have sinned," the voice said through Sally's mouth.

"Why is she talking like Rabbi Weiss?" Eric asked.

"I *am* Rabbi Weiss, you nincompoop," the voice said.

"Ezra?" Janice gasped.

Eric took the remote control and turned off the television. He smirked.

"Rabbi Weiss is dead."

"I am dead," the voice agreed.

"Nice trick, Sally," he said. "Where'd you learn it?"

"I am in pain!" the voice wailed so loudly that Eric took a step backwards.

"Why are you in pain?" Janice cried.

"We have sinned, Janice, we have sinned," the voice said, in a fade out. Suddenly Sally's face loosened. She shook herself and looked angrily at her brother.

"Why'd you turn the TV off?"

Eric looked at his mother.

"Sally?" he said. "Do Rabbi Weiss again."

"Do what?"

"You know, do Rabbi Weiss. Imitate him, like you just did."

"Rabbi Weiss? He's dead." Sally reminded him with a sarcastic smile.

***

Janice had not yet found a new job. Her experience was not in demand by Cleveland synagogues since the whole community knew she'd betrayed her husband with a late rabbi. She had no income, and Joel, who'd always been the major breadwinner, wasn't sending any, although his lawyer was paying Eric's math tutor and Sally's clarinet teacher. A couple times the lawyer had also arranged for the children to meet their father somewhere in town. Janice took a loan from her mother and had her lawyer tell Joel's lawyer that the kids were going to starve this way. Eric was skipping school and coming home every night way after midnight. Sally no longer smiled, although she seemed to be trying hard to pretend that nothing had changed. Janice was not sleeping at nights. On top of all that, her mother came to visit.

The next possession took place at the kitchen table at dinner on the same day her mother arrived. Eric was out who-knows-where with friends and Sally wasn't talking. Janice had just dished out brisket and potatoes, and her mom was at her for not keeping Eric in line. Suddenly Sally stiffened again and her face froze. The same voice spoke, groaning.

"I have sinned!"

Janice's mom looked at Sally and smiled comfortingly. "No, you haven't, dear."

"I, Ezra Weiss, have sinned!" the voice thundered.

"Rabbi Ezra Weiss?" Janice's mom asked suspiciously.

"Mrs. Persky, it's always a pleasure to see you in Cleveland," Rabbi Weiss's voice said to her.

"Is it really you?" Janice's mom inquired. "I just want to make sure before I give you a piece of my mind."

"Unfortunately, my soul will be allowed no rest and will wander this world until I receive the forgiveness of those I have wronged," Rabbi Weiss explained. "And I have been allowed to possess the body of poor young Sally so that I might endeavor to arrange the necessary penance."

"You are a ghost possessing my granddaughter?" the grandmother said.

"Indeed," said Rabbi Weiss.

"Ridiculous. You're a Reform rabbi. You don't believe in demonic possession." Janice's mom had grown up in a traditional home and had attended a Conservative synagogue all her life. While she had shed most of her childhood observances, she considered Reform Jews to be just this side of heresy.

"It really is embarrassing," Rabbi Weiss admitted. "Totally irrational and opposed to everything I ever believed."

"Serves you right for seducing my daughter. Wander the world forever. Just leave my Sally alone," Janice's mom hissed.

"What must I do?" Janice asked, as if mesmerized. The half of her soul that was a circle of light blazed. The amoeba was squirming.

"I need to talk to Linda."

"So go possess one of her kids and talk to her," Janice's mom suggested.

"I'm afraid the rules don't allow that."

"What rules?"

"There are rules here. It's hard to explain."

"But Ezra," Janice said, almost in tears, "I can't call Linda."

"If you ever loved me, you must," Rabbi Weiss said plaintively as the voice faded out once again. Sally's face relaxed. She blinked and put her hands to her belly.

"May I be excused?" Sally asked. "I feel funny."

"Wait," her grandmother commanded. Then, to Janice: "What's the number?" She got up from the table and picked up the wall phone.

"What number?" Janice whispered.

"The Weiss's."

"Mom, no."

"I'm not going to have my granddaughter taken over by a rabbi who shtups the whole Temple staff," the mother said. "Let's get this over with."

"471-6089," said Sally, staring at her brisket gravy.

Mom dialed. There was a click.

"Linda? Hello. It's Bella Persky."

Silence on the other end, then a few words.

"No, I've just come for a visit. I have a very important request for you. I need you to come over to Janice's house right away."

The words on the other end were harsh and abrupt.

"We have had a communication from Ezra."

Linda spoke some unspeakable words. Then there was a click.

"She hung up," said Bella.

Sally pointed to her gravy. "An arrow. She'll come."

Fifteen minutes later, while Bella was doing the dishes, there was a knock on the door.

"I'll get it," said Sally.

She escorted Linda Weiss up to the kitchen. Linda looked warily at Janice, who was still seated, like a zombie, at the table.

Bella wiped her hands on a dishtowel.

"Coffee?"

"Please," said Linda.

"Sit down."

Bella made coffee for the adults and cinnamon tea for Sally. She took some of Sally's birthday cookies out of the freezer, put them in the microwave for a minute, and placed them in the middle of the table. She sat down.

"Sally?"

"Wait, I'll just go to the bathroom first." Sally ran upstairs.

"What's going on?" Linda asked Bella. She ignored Janice.

"This is not going to be easy, but I think we can settle everything relatively quickly," Bella reassured her. Sally returned, sat down next to Linda, and folded her hands in her lap.

"Okay, I'm ready," she said to no one in particular. Her face tightened and contorted again. Linda drew back.

"I have sinned!" Rabbi Weiss's voice moaned again.

Linda looked at Bella. Bella nudged her.

"It's Ezra."

"Ezra, is that you?" Linda asked Sally.

"I have sinned!" Rabbi Weiss said again.

"Of course you have. First you died and left me to raise four teenagers all by myself, and then during the shiva, I got the news that you'd been sleeping with this snotrag of an executive director of yours," Linda said sternly.

"I have been doomed to wander the earth. My soul will have no rest until I obtain your forgiveness."

"Why should I forgive you?" asked Linda. "What have you done to deserve it?"

"I made a horrible error," Ezra said to her. "I betrayed what was most dear to me. It's all my fault. You can't blame Janice."

"See!" Bella whispered triumphantly.

"I was the one who came on to her. Joel was putting in long hours with dead bodies in the hospital morgue and she was lonely. We were alone in the building and I could not resist temptation."

Linda was silent.

"I never betrayed you before, in twenty-six years of marriage. Remember how much we loved each other. How much we loved our children."

Linda began to weep. "Then what happened? Was something wrong with me?"

Rabbi Weiss choked up. "I felt I was getting old. Like my soul was going stale. I liked my job, I loved my family, but somehow that love wasn't buoyant any more. That first evening, when I found myself alone with Janice in her office, my soul broke free and began to ascend. I knew I should tie it down again, that I would lose all I held dear. But it kept slipping away. I followed its ascent and it led me into her arms."

"You should suffer forever," Linda said bitterly. She looked at Janice. "Both of you."

"I would like to point out," Bella said, "that this marital squabble of yours is taking place at the expense of my granddaughter. She has a right to a normal childhood. Adolescence is tough enough when your parents are getting divorced. The last thing she needs is to be possessed by a dead rabbi."

"Ezra?" Janice said softly.

"Yes, Janice?"

"It's my fault. I should have said no."

"You were weak. I took advantage of you."

"But did you love her?" Linda asked quietly.

"I never stopped loving you," Ezra insisted.

"But did you love her?"

The voice remained silent. Janice thought that it had gone again, but Sally's face remained contorted.

"I loved her." And then: "I loved her more."

Janice began to cry. "I loved you, too."

"You always told me that in this day and age, in the last decade of the twentieth century, we know there is no individual life after death." Linda laughed.

"You call this a life?" Ezra Weiss wailed. "Time moves differently here. It's much slower."

"Why did you do it?" Linda demanded to know.

"How can I explain it? I saw a fire in Janice's soul. It burned so bright! I couldn't live without it. My soul split in two. Half belonged to you, and half to Janice."

Linda turned to Janice. "How did you seduce him?"

"I didn't seduce him!" Janice exclaimed. "But my soul was also divided. Part of it remained with Joel, but the fiery part sought out Ezra."

Linda considered for a moment. "If you loved her with only half your soul, I only have to forgive that half?"

Ezra considered a moment. "I suppose so."

"And the other half?"

"The other half will wait for you to join me."

"Is that a promise?" Linda wept.

"It is," said Rabbi Weiss.

"Then I forgive that faithless half of your soul," Linda said, "on condition that it remain bound to the fire you saw in Janice."

The voice fell silent. After a moment, it said, "Just a second while I check this out."

A couple minutes passed, during which Sally's face relaxed but her normal expression did not return. Then she tensed again.

"Look, I asked and here's what we can do. You've each forgiven your halves of my soul. I can go to heaven on that basis. Linda's got a place reserved because she's blameless. Half of Janice's soul comes with me now and half stays with her until her time comes."

"That's very selfish," Bella said. "Are you sure you're going to heaven?"

"I'm a rabbi," Ezra pointed out.

"I'm sure there's whole congregations of rabbis in hell," Bella said.

"Jews don't believe in hell," said Rabbi Ezra Weiss.

"You didn't believe in heaven, either," said Bella.

"Well, I believed in a general concept of unification with God."

"Shut up already," Bella advised.

"If it will be good for Linda, I consent," Janice whispered.

"You're letting him fool you again," Bella shouted.

"I consent," Janice said.

***

Sally did not see signs in egg yolks after that, and she was never possessed again by a dead rabbi. Janice and Joel negotiated a joint custody agreement but the children showed a clear preference for their father, who eventually won possession of the house. Janice found a job as a secretary in a law firm. She disliked the work, which was monotonous, but it paid the bills. She got up in the mornings, went to work, came home, cooked dinner, watched television, and went to bed. Eric and then Sally graduated from high school, then from college, then got married and had children. Bella died. Janice eventually left the law firm and moved into a retirement community. Once when she was visiting Sally, she brought up the subject again.

"How do you explain it?" she asked her daughter.

Sally shrugged. "I don't know. I've never given it much thought."

"Did you make it up? Was it a game? A trick you and your brother played on me?"

Sally grew impatient, almost angry. "Mom, stop it. Was it such an important thing in your life?"

"My life," said Janice, "has always been the same since."

Passacaglia

A hand passed before my face and I was jerked out of my reverie. An almost chilly breeze was blowing from Bethlehem. The muffled sound of the wedding band, playing Levantine-tinged pop settings of verses from the Song of Songs and Jeremiah, filtered through the glass doors, blaring for a few seconds whenever a child ran in or out.

The face to which the hand was connected belonged to Vardit, the bride's best friend. Unlike Aviya, whose demure pearl-white dress reached to the floor and had sleeves below the elbow, Vardit was sleeveless and in red. Her arms and face glowed from dancing.

"Bored?"

I removed the buds from my ears. "I needed a break," I said.

"I needed some air." She removed a pack of cigarettes from a small macramé bag she had slung over her shoulder and jokingly offered me one. I leaned back against a marble-faced pillar and surveyed the Judean hills. On this hill in southern Jerusalem, you can see the Dead Sea on a clear day. At night, the hills to the southeast are dark shadows, but most of the panorama is alive with the lights of Arab cities and Jewish neighborhoods.

"You look a little sad."

"So do you."

She took a long drag. "Well, I'm losing my best friend," she said.

I looked at her in surprise. "You think?"

"It's never the same after a wedding, is it?"

"I'm sure it will be different. That doesn't mean it won't be, though."

She looked at me. "It's not just Matan. I have other friends with boyfriends. But he's taken her.... Well, she's very different this past year."

"You mean the religious stuff?"

"She's so *spiritual*." Her arms fluttered. "I mean, we both grew up with Shabbat and holidays and kashrut at all that. That's hard enough. But all these gematriyot and sefirot and kavanot. It's not Matan who's standing between us, it's the Shekhinah."

"There are fifty gates to the Torah." I smiled. "That's not the one I choose to go through, but if that's what she and Matan get into...."

"The fact is that I really am losing patience with the whole thing. All these rules. And it's all based on this primitive book that has nothing to do with our lives today."

The wedding band suddenly drowned us out. A kid in an untucked purple shirt held the door open, looking around. When he saw Vardit, he did a leap over the three steps leading up to the garden where we sat and ran up to her.

"Hey, Vardit, I've been looking all over for you. Why aren't you dancing?"

"How would you know?" she said. "Have you been looking over the divider at the girls? That's not allowed!"

"Come back in," he urged her, as if nothing in the universe was more important than for her to return to the dance floor.

"I'll be there in a minute, when I finish smoking," she said. He gave her a smile as wide as the summer night, leapt back down the steps, and ran back into the hall.

She watched him as he went. "Everyone's telling me 'You're next!' But I don't want to be next."

"So don't be."

"Sometimes I think love is, well, so *conventional*, if you know what I mean. Why should I have to get married?"

"I can only recommend it," I said, "from my own experience."

She turned back to me suddenly. "In synagogue, on Shabbat, I was reading the Torah portion. Did you read it? I get the feeling that everyone is just mumbling the words. If they paid attention to what they mean, they'd vomit. You know what it says? If someone worships other gods, you should kill him. If he violates the Sabbath, kill him. If he disobeys any law in the Torah, kill him. Who wants to worship a God who's so worried about the competition that he needs to use murder to keep his people in line?"

"So we should throw out the Torah and find a different sacred book?"

"We don't think that way today." She shrugged. "So why keep reading it?"

"Your question reminds me of the music I was listening to when you interrupted me."

"I'm so sorry," she said with a laugh. "What was it?"

"I was in the middle of the fourth movement of Brahms Fourth Symphony in E minor."

"I remember Brahms from school. We spent a couple weeks on him in music class."

"Did you like him?"

"I think I did. But I haven't listened to much classical music since. You know, it's not cool in the army. So I'm not sure I remember. Wasn't he, well, retro? I seem to remember the teacher saying that he was a nineteenth-century throwback to the classical age."

"Want to listen?" I asked, handing her the buds.

She took out Kleenex, wiped them off, and put them in her ears. I restarted the movement and she listened intently for a couple minutes and then motioned for me to stop.

"Sad," she said, freeing up her right ear. "But it doesn't seem to hold together. Isn't there supposed to be one main theme or two? This seems to start something new every few measures."

"You're right," I said. "We expect a symphony's fourth movement to be in sonata form, where two themes play off against each other, or rondo form, with a catchy theme that keeps coming back. Brahms is doing something different here. Listen some more. Concentrate on the background, the bass line and the harmony below the melodies."

She listened some more.

"There's something that keeps going." In a clear voice, she sang five slow notes. "Something like that."

"Very good. That's called the ground bass. It repeats thirty times, one after the other, below the other melodies. It's always there."

"Ground bass?" She wrinkled her face. "Doesn't that something have to do with Bach? Like the Goldberg Variations? I remember Hagit teaching us that."

"Precisely. So here Brahms isn't a throwback to the Classical era, which was just two generations before him. He's going further back, to Bach and the Baroque."

"What for? Didn't he want to do something new?"

"Well, it was new. No one before him had thought to write a symphonic movement based on a Baroque procedure. See, this movement is a passacaglia, a Baroque form in which a continually innovative melodic line sounds over a repeated background theme. It's the background that holds all that innovation together."

She put the bud back in her ear and motioned for me to click the Ipod. She listened intently to the end, and then handed the earphones back to me.

"Is that a tear in your eye?" I said.

"That flute solo." She nodded, wiping the tear away with a Kleenex.

"He even stole the theme from Bach. Just tweaked it slightly to fit his needs," I told her.

The wedding band blasted again. The kid in the purple shirt bounded out the door. He caught Vardit's eyes, did a flourish with his arms, and this time jumped up the steps backwards.

"So?" he said. "Are you coming?"

"Can't you see I'm having a deep conversation?" she said with mock seriousness.

He held out his hand to me. "Deep is great," he said. "But now?" After we shook, he placed his hand lightly on Vardit's wrist and pulled her up. "Come on!"

She gently removed his hand from hers and smoothed out her dress. "I'll be right there. I promise."

"I give you two minutes," he said over his shoulder, running back into the hall. "If I don't see you, I'll have to bring reinforcements!"

"Brahms had a great love. An older woman," I said. "Clara Schumann, piano virtuoso and the widow of Robert."

"She married two great composers?"

"No, because Brahms refused. He was afraid, it seems, to love."

Vardit seemed to be considering this.

"So what you were saying before. "I think I get the point," she said. "God is in the ground bass?"

"To improvise well, you need a foundation. You need something in the background to hold you. Without a centuries-old melody and structure behind you, you can't move forward. Not in any real, constructive way."

"Didn't he want to do something new?"

"He did something new by adapting something old."

"And what about slaughtering the non-believers?"

"From the very beginning, the Torah hasn't been just the written word," I reminded her. "The written word is the repeating theme in the background, but each new generation of sages and rabbis and believers—and non-believers, too—produce new variations. I don't think that even the craziest fundamentalist in this century—and God knows we've got some crazy ones—takes those injunctions seriously."

"So why do we need to read them year after year?"

"If you hadn't heard them on Shabbat, if you hadn't been horrified about what you heard, we wouldn't be having this conversation."

"And we wouldn't be having it if I hadn't found you here outside listening to old people's music either."

The band boomed again. She looked at the door, which was being held open by the kid in the purple shirt. He had two friends behind him.

"Oh, he's such a pain." She sighed. "I'd better go in."

"Maybe I'll come with you. It looks like you might need protection."

She laughed. "Just one more thing. Do you think that's why Brahms wrote something so sad? Because he gave up an opportunity to love?"

"I can only guess," I said, although I don't know if she heard me. By the time I finished my sentence, she'd been swept off to the dance floor.

Peripheral Vision

When Hanan felt someone's gaze on his Android, his first instinct was to tip it to the left to avoid intrusion. His second instinct was to tip it to the right to offer a better view. It was, after all, a fine and beautiful photograph of Yael, and while intimacy demanded a certain level of privacy, pride demanded a certain level of public display.

In an earlier age, perhaps, privacy would have won out, but in an earlier age, he would not be gazing at a photograph of his girlfriend on an electronic device in the crowded waiting room of the Terem all-night emergency clinic in Talpiot. Were he, say, a member of Trumpeldor's Labor Brigades back in pioneering days, one who had been taken on muleback to a doctor's home in Yavne'el (had it been founded then?), because of, say, a burn on his shin from a misaimed bucket of hot asphalt, he would have had to conjure up Yael's bare limbs in his mind's eye and no one would have been able to peek. That body would have been his alone to see. But then no one else would know what a treasure he had and, let's face it, part of the enjoyment of a treasure is the admiration of others.

It took only a fraction of a second for him to make out in his peripheral vision that the invasive but welcome gaze came from a small person dressed in a long-sleeve shirt, plaid with wide blue stripes, tucked into brown corduroy trousers with an elastic waistband. Above the eye was a black velvet kipah, and the head to which it belonged leaned lightly and lovingly on the forearm of a lean and tall man in a black suit and clipped beard with an open book on his lap from which he was reading aloud.

The boy dutifully turned his eyes to the book, but not for long. Hanan gave him a smile. The boy shifted in his chair and smiled cautiously back.

"Tomorrow this sign shall come to pass," the father intoned, pointing to the page and glancing at his son. "The Ben Ish Hai is talking here about a verse from the story of the plagues in Egypt. But we know that the word 'sign' doesn't have to be a bad thing, a bunch of flies that got in the Egyptians' beds and food and noses. A sign is also the mitzvot, the commandments that God has given the Jews, which are a sign of the covenant between the Holy One, Blessed be He, and his people." He explained how if you rearrange the Hebrew letters of the word "tomorrow," which are MHR, you get RMH, which is the number 248, which is the number of limbs and organs of the human body, and also the number of positive injunctions in the Torah.

"How do we know there are that many?" the boy asked his father.

"We can count them in the Torah, like our Sages did," the father replied.

"No, I mean the parts of the body."

"Well, if you look at a person's body, if you could see everything about it, you could count that many."

"Let's count," said the boy, pointing to the photograph on Hanan's phone. The father looked. Here Hanan's first instinct took control, but not quickly enough for the father not to see. He put his hand gently on the boy's head and addressed Hanan.

"She's very beautiful." This gave Hanan a warm feeling inside. He felt like calling Yael right then and there to tell her. But maybe that wouldn't be a good idea.

"There's certainly a lot to count there," the father said to his son. "But we wouldn't get to 248 because we can't see what's inside." He said to Hanan: "What brings you here?"

Hanan rolled up the right leg of his jeans and pointed to the swollen and scabbed purple spot there. "Infected cut. From my bicycle. And you?"

"Kfir has been wheezing all day," he said, his eyes on the boy. "We thought he just needed to rest, but it got worse after supper." They exchanged names. His was Shlomi Biton.

"Sorry to distract him," Hanan said.

"Well, you're in love," Shlomi observed. "It's like the verse we have over the ark: 'I place my love before me always.' Although without the picture."

"We've been together since just last week," Hanan said, happy to have someone to tell his story to. "She's amazing."

"I'm sure she is."

"We met in the line at the supermarket, isn't that something?" He thought a minute. "I guess that's different for you. You probably didn't meet your wife in the supermarket."

"No," Shlomi said.

"I guess you get matched up by your parents, or your rabbi, or something," Hanan quickly added: "Which is fine with me, if that's what you like." Then he added again: "But there's something exciting about it—you know, chance, fate."

"When I met Mazal," Shlomi shrugged. "it was definitely a roll of the dice. Yes, the head of my yeshiva told me she was my intended, but until you meet the girl, you don't know. In fact, she was working just down the street here, at Bank Hapoalim."

"Ah, so you're from this area?"

"Sure," Shlomi told him. "Went to the Masorti high school up the hill here."

"Really?" Hanan said. "That's where Yael went." He thought a minute. "I guess we're about the same age. Even if you have a kid."

"Three." Shlomi smiled. "You're a student?"

"Yeah, computer science and Israeli history double major, second year."

"Nice combination." He looked at his son. "It's just that after fooling around and wasting my time in high school on girls and parties and hashish, I decided that I wanted a life of Torah."

"I guess that means that Kfir won't meet his love by chance," Hanan laughed.

"Why shouldn't his mother and I decide for him?" Shlomi said, with a deadpan expression that seemed both ironic and serious. "After all, we know him better than he knows himself."

"Still, maybe he should have the chance you had," Hanan suggested. "You know, to go to high school, hang out with girls. Then he could decide himself about the yeshiva stuff."

"Why leave it to chance? Sometimes it works, but a lot of times it causes a lot of pain."

Hanan couldn't disagree, given some of his previous experiences. He shrugged. "Pain's part of the game. It seems wrong to me to close off your kid's options."

"It seems wrong to me to have a picture like that of Yael on your phone," Shlomi shot back.

"Why is she naked?" Kfir asked.

"Well, she's very beautiful," Hanan said. "So I want to look at her all the time. Anyway, she's not quite naked."

"Pretty close," the boy said.

"Yeah, pretty close," Hanan agreed.

"You know the Ben Ish Hai?" Shlomi asked. "That's what we're reading." He pointed to the book and his eyes asked for his son's attention. If you play with the letters more, you get RHM, which means "womb," he explained, symbolizing the love between God and his people and the love between one Jew and another.

"And the Ben Ish Hai says that every Jew is required to perform the 248 mitzvot, but how can every person perform so many mitzvot? So he says that we can do RMH through RHM, mitzvot through love. Because, say, there are mitzvot that you can't do, but your friend can do, and through the love between you, the mitzvot your friend does become your mitzvot and the ones you do become his. And so through love we all do all the mitzvot."

The boy looked intently at the book, but Hanan could tell that out of the corner of his eye he saw the phone as well.

"Like him and Yael?" Kfir asked, pointing at Hanan. "They do mitzvot together?"

"I'm sure they do," Shlomi said.

"Ben-Ami! Come in please," a male nurse in scrubs called out in an Arab accent.

"That's me," Hanan said, slipping the phone into his pocket.

"May you enjoy a full and speedy recovery!" Shlomi said. Then to Kfir: "Don't worry, it'll be our turn soon."

The nurse joked with Hanan about bike falls and impressing girls as he took blood pressure, temperature, and oxygen level. He then told Hanan to return to the waiting room.

Shlomi and Kfir were still there, but they had their hands over their faces and were mumbling something. Hanan sat down next to them. Soon they finished and uncovered their eyes. Shlomi's face had changed. He seemed distracted, sad. The boy sat quietly, staring into space, as if he had absorbed his father's distress.

"We were just reciting the Shema," Shlomi said, his words spaced more widely than before. "It's late and I'm afraid Kfir will fall asleep on the way home and not get to say it before bedtime."

"Biton!" It was the nurse at the door. Shlomi touched Kfir lightly on the shoulder and motioned at the door.

"You know," he said to Kfir. "In the Shema, there are 248 letters. And the Ben Ish Hai says that's why it stands for all the other mitzvot together, and also for love, as we say we love our God with all our heart and all our soul and all our might."

Kfir got slowly to his feet, thinking deeply. "So it is also like Yael's body?"

Shlomi took his son's hand and looked straight into Hanan's eyes. "Yes, it is very much like Yael," he said to him. "Please give her my love, will you? And tell her I am sorry." And he led Kfir quickly through the door.

Hanan could not respond for a second, and when he did, Shlomi was not there to hear.

"So you know her?" he said, his mouth dry. And he realized that when Shlomi saw the photograph on his phone, it was not the first time he had seen Yael unclothed.

The Dryad

She laughed at how easy it had been not to think about it, how well her plan had gone. Her companions were no longer visible ahead. Soon they'd wonder about her and send someone back in search. In the meantime, she'd have something to eat. She unrolled the clingy plastic from around her sandwich, which had been squeezed by the weight of her water bottles into a shape that might have been a heart but wasn't. Down below, raucous teenagers gamboled in a spring that seemed to be the source of the river along which she and her companions had hiked all morning.

The rains had not yet come, yet the Tzipori River flowed gently along the terraced channel that she and the rest of the group had walked along that morning. At one point it bowed and nearly circled a low hill on which a tiny village perched. Children played in a schoolyard. The leader had given the village a name she could no longer remember. Further on was an old millhouse you could now rent out for weddings and bar mitzvahs. There the trail had crossed the river (all of three meters wide) and she had followed the others over half-submerged stones. The water, which the leader said was partly sewage, washed over her boots. Last to cross, she had probed the riverbed with her poles to steady herself. She thought of turning back but did not.

She hadn't hiked seriously since her teenage scout years, which were three decades past by now. Back then, at tough spots, like the river crossing, the boys were always ready and eager to help. Some were very serious about it, as if pulling her up a boulder or guiding her over a narrow spot in a path above a canyon was the very reason they had been placed on this earth. Others had laughed at her fears, in a big-brotherly way (she was the oldest in her family, and had always wanted a big brother). In this group, today, the others were obliging but cool.

She signed up for the hike because she knew it would be good for her. She didn't need a psychologist to tell her that sitting at home and brooding would only cast her deeper into her abyss. And while her friends were sympathetic and always ready to lend an ear, she felt she needed to get away, to be with people who did not know her story, who could see her as she was, that is, as she had been, as she was now but for that. Getting out into nature also seemed like a good idea, getting out into nature, that is, without a hundred screaming twelve-year-olds, as she did when she chaperoned the fifth and sixth-grade class trip each year. So she looked on the Nature Protection Society website and found a Saturday hike, one in the category of not-so-difficult, but long enough, at several hours, to ensure that families with small children would mostly likely not sign up.

The late November morning had not yet dawned when her alarm woke her up. The room was freezing and she quickly slipped into the old pair of pants, t-shirt, and sweatshirt she'd placed on her bedside table. She washed her face at the kitchen sink and turned on the electric kettle. As it boiled, she opened the refrigerator to remove the sandwich and bag of vegetables she prepared the night before. She'd talked to the leader on Friday just to make sure she was properly equipped and he'd said to bring half as much food as she thought she'd need. So all she added to the refrigerator stash was a small plastic box filled with raisins and walnuts. Two empty Nestea bottles filled with water, hat, sunscreen, and extra pair of socks were already in the small backpack she always used for school hikes. There'd still be room to stuff in the sweatshirt and jacket when the day grew warmer, as it was forecast to do. She ladled a heaping spoonful of

Tasters Choice into her thermos cup, poured on the boiling water, added milk, stirred, and screwed it shut. Then she took her bag, opened the door, closed it behind her quietly, and locked it slowly, so as not to awaken those who were still sleeping.

It took her nearly two hours to reach the meeting spot, a shopping center next to Kibbutz Yagur, at the foot of Mt. Carmel (she'd taken a wrong turn at Yokne'am that got her caught in morning traffic, but thankfully not for long). The group was all she had hoped for. The leader was a thirtyish wiry outdoors type with a ratty Australian hat over his disordered curls. There was an older, white-haired couple who spoke English with a German accent and who looked like they had scaled many an Alp together in their time. A trio of energetic and talkative women with guttural hets and ayins explained that they'd been doing this for years to get some time away from their husbands and homes. Finally, a quiet, morose-looking guy of about forty. The leader had everyone say their names in sequence, and she immediately forgot them. He made sure they all had enough water and money to take the bus back from the endpoint of the hike, then had them get back in their cars and drive a short way after him to the trail head.

This section of the Israel Trail passed first through a moshav, then headed out into the wild, up an incline into hilly terrain where occasional olive groves appeared in the midst of meadows. She chatted with her companions. It felt entirely natural for her not to tell them why, in fact, she was with them, and even when they asked her about her family, she didn't even have to think first before formulating an answer that elegantly avoided the thing she had chosen to leave out of this adventure. But the others were in better shape and she soon found herself falling behind. Every so often they waited up for her but, increasingly, she walked alone, a few dozen paces behind them.

At one point they disappeared around a spur and she felt a pang of fear, but as soon as she rounded the bend, she saw them standing and admiring a large and low-branching oak that stood like a shrine in the center of a triangular plateau between two hills. It was a venerable tree that had cast many acorns on the grass, where a few early lavender-pale cyclamens were flowering. The trunk was knurled and had a large crevice lined with smooth bark that looked like a pair of lips. As the others gazed, she cast down her poles, strode over to the tree, and inserted herself into the opening. Her hips were really too wide, but, laughing, she managed to get in almost up to her waist. The others laughed, too, except for the morose man, who looked the other way.

The leader asked her how it felt and he told them about dryads, the nymphs that resided in oak trees, and who lived only so long as their tree did. For the ancient Greeks, chopping down an oak tree was tantamount to bringing a horrible curse upon oneself, he said. In addition to killing the tree, you were killing the dryad.

She told them that she indeed felt herself to be an integral part of the tree. As if they were one flesh, as if she were herself a branch and about to sprout acorns.

The leader urged them to move on as there was quite a way to go still. The sun was now high in the sky, so she removed her sweatshirt and stuffed it on top of the jacket in her backpack before they descended into the river valley where rippling water harmonized with birdsong. They remained together until the river crossing, when the others again moved ahead of her and she could barely see them in the distance. She decided it was time for a break. Let them come back and find her.

A girl screamed in the spring below and two boys shouted back and forth. After eating half her sandwich, she opened up the remaining half and ate it as she used to eat the ones she took on scout hikes—picking out the pepper and cucumber, then eating the cheese, and finally each side of the roll, one after the other. The sun had gone behind a cloud. She thought about putting her sweatshirt back on, but once she began walking again she'd warm up, so it probably wasn't worth it. Out of the corner of her eye, she caught sight of a figure down the path, just at the bend far ahead where her companions had vanished. She did not look. It waited there a moment, then began to walk toward her. She gazed down at the spring. She soon saw that it was, as she expected, the leader, who called out to her. She turned her head to look at him but did not get up. He approached and called her the dryad asked if everything was ok, if she needed help. She laughed and said everything was just fine, she had just needed some rest and refueling. The girl down at the spring, or maybe another girl, screamed again.

He held out his arm and she grabbed it and he pulled her up from her rock. Hadn't it been nice, he asked, back then in Greece, when a lonely wanderer could stop by an oak tree and have a chat with a nymph? She replied: And back when a nymph could be so much a part of a tree that they died together, wasn't there something wonderful about that as well? He looked at her strangely, and then agreed that there was. They walked on and rejoined the group, where she told them all about her sandwich, and the spring below, but nothing about why she'd come. Which felt perfectly natural.

A Him to him

It's spring in Jerusalem. Fields, yards, and the few vacant lots that remain in this overbuilt city are burgeoning with blood-red anemones. Two weeks ago, Ilana and I visited a hill not too far away. It was carpeted with purple lupines and growing over the ruins of an ancient city. The flowers perfume the air and after each of the rainy season's concluding drizzles, the soil smells alive.

Perhaps spring came late in Leipzig in 1727. How else to explain the sorrow of that opening chord in the organ and strings, the melody that rises, then falls as if it can go on no longer, only to rise again? Why, if your Redeemer died for your sins, did you sigh rather than celebrate? Why, if the equinox had passed and the day was longer than the night, did you have the choir, entering just as the instrumental melody comes to rest, stun me with a wail of helplessness, of hopelessness, "Come ye daughters, share my lament—see him!"

Yes, I know, "Him," with a capital H. A big Him for you, a little him for me.

I should tell you up front that I don't believe in Jesus. No, I don't believe that God the Father sent his only begotten Son to suffer for the sins of humankind. I don't believe that the Messiah was crucified, only to rise on the third day, nor do I believe that he will come again. I have only respect for Christians for whom the passion of Christ inspires love and good works. But it's not my story. I come from a different tradition. Gods who turn into men seem, well, a little suspicious to us Jews, just like humans who claim to be God. In the sixth decade of my life, I now know that religions and belief systems do not compel moral choices. They leave us to make the same moral choices we'd have to make even without them. The sacred colors our world but does not compel the colors we see; those who can hear the music of the divine experience life differently from the tone-deaf, but they must still decide what sort of music to attend to. Men and women of my faith have used the teachings of our prophets and rabbis to further hatred and iniquity, while others have used them to further love and benevolence. Your teacher Luther set the Germans against the Jews, but he also inspired your music. I do not forgive him his evil, but I value the good.

I seem to have gone off track. What I mean to say is that you wrote the *Matthew Passion* as you prepared yourself spiritually for the rejection, humiliation, and agony of your Lord. As you turned your despair to music, the Jews in Leipzig (they'd only recently been allowed back, after being expelled 300 years previously) were preparing to leave slavery for freedom, Egypt for the Promised Land. This, perhaps the greatest of your choral works, will be performed here in Jerusalem and throughout the world on Good Friday, which this year falls during our Passover week. And the way the calendars work out, that evening my family and I will be saying kaddish, the mourner's prayer, for my son. That's son, with a small s. His name was Niot and he died two years ago. Like the apostles with Jesus, the Seder night was the last I had with him. Since then your music, which I have often listened to at the start of spring, sounds much different.

"Whither is my beloved gone?" the Daughter of Zion laments. "Where has your friend departed?" the chorus replies.

I have to admit that for many years I did not really understand why you were so upset. After all, it happened so long ago, and don't you all believe that Jesus is with you always? If the whole purpose of the incarnation was that Jesus die on the cross, shouldn't you be positively joyful that he accomplished his mission so successfully?

But no one can listen to your music and think that you are pretending, that this mourning of Christ is mere ritual. I am reminded of a homily that often comes up on Seder night. We say, as part of that ceremony, that each of us must view him or herself as having personally participated in the Exodus from Egypt. Maimonides adds a single letter to this statement and changes its meaning—he says that each of us "must *show* himself to have participated in the Exodus." That is, not just go through the dry rituals prescribed for the Seder but actually feel so strongly within that he is a freed slave that it will be evident to all those who look at him.

So you must show, you must sing your sorrow. Still, the resurrection is soon to follow. The gloom of Good Friday dissipates on Easter Sunday. Knowing that you would be rejoicing with Jesus on the day after the morrow, how sadly should you sing on Friday?

What I wouldn't give for a resurrection on the third day, or after the second year.

You end this Passion with a chorus that recalls the grief of the organ and strings at the beginning. True, the formerly minor harmonies are now major, but there is no happiness here—the feeling is more one of resignation. "Sleep in peace, sleep Thou in the Father's breast," says the libretto. There's no indication from the voices and instruments that he will ever live again. Elsewhere the words speak of the redemption, but even where they do, your music never fully rejoices. I know that feeling—the sense that every joy that comes my way is incomplete, that a hole yawns in the middle of every happiness.

That's what I hear now in the *Matthew Passion*. What I now hear, what I didn't hear before my own loss, is that Jesus is not just a Him for you. He is also a him. The resurrection is a fine mystery for the immortal soul, but it is solace only for the spirit. In your Passion's music—no matter what the formal doctrine expressed in the libretto states—the Christ who reappeared on Sunday as the Son of God was not the Jesus murdered on Friday. The man who died on Friday was a son and a friend. The incarnation of God who appeared on Sunday was neither. Jesus had come again, but Mary did not have the child she had suckled, nurtured, and taught, nor did James and Peter and the other apostles have the brother and companion they had studied, traveled, and eaten with. Your music says that the world, perhaps, was saved, but it was a world in which those who had known Jesus the man were still grieving, and would grieve for the rest of their lives.

Our family's season of mourning does not end on the third day. We say kaddish on Pesach, but we will visit his grave only two weeks later. (In Jewish tradition, Nissan, the month of the Exodus, is a joyful one, so memorial services are put off.) A few days after that, we will ascend again to the Mt. Herzl military cemetery to mark Memorial Day, for Niot was a soldier when he died. We will bid him farewell, knowing that he will not come again. But in your music I hear that, on the most fundamental human level, the brute fact that Niot will not return to me, Ilana, to his brother and sisters, to his friends, is no different from the fact that Jesus, the son of God, reappeared on earth, but no longer as the son of man. Herr Bach, I listen to your music and know that you felt the loss of Jesus as if it were the loss of your very own son. And you lost ten of your own children. I cannot imagine the grief I feel raised by an order of magnitude.

In the wake of my loss, the sublime music of your *Matthew Passion* has taught me something. There is theology, which concerns God, and there is anthropology, which concerns human beings. I appreciate, in a way I never could before, the power and attraction of a theology centered on the loss of a son. After all, until not long ago, it was an experience, a tragedy, a rupture that nearly every family underwent. Yet what I hear in your music is not a grief for a lost God. It is the devastation not of God the father but of Johann Sebastian Bach the father, who has lost so many sons and daughters, for each of whom he grieves for the rest of his life. For that father, there is no consolation in the resurrection of the Son of God, only resignation and acceptance. Spring may be here, the flowers may bloom in the Promised Land, the soil may be moist and warm and ready to produce life, but we, you and I, your family and mine, your surviving children and mine, feel only aching love and yearning for the human, for those children, images of God and of their parents, left behind in their graves in Egypt or nailed to the cross.

PART III: TWINKLING
IN THE DARK

The Plowman Meets the Reaper

Behold, days are coming, says the Lord, when the plowman shall overtake the reaper, and the treader of grapes him who sows seed ... And I will bring back the captivity of my people of Israel, and they shall build the wasted cities, and inhabit them; they shall also make gardens, and eat their fruit. (Amos 9:13–14)

He knew her, she lived past the sands, in the part of Rassco where you heard German and the Philharmonic when the windows were open. He sometimes went to play soccer on the street there when he needed to get away from home. Her house, one of the tiny two-room cubicles that made up the neighborhood, had a small garden that looked as if she went out every morning to straighten and polish each leaf and petal. He'd often see her sitting on her front stoop with one or another lady friend, both in high heels, in long sleeves even on the hottest days of summer. Sometimes she would have a brush in hand and an easel in front of her, painting scenes of a city that looked nothing like Holon.

Once he passed by and she wasn't outside and he felt so disappointed that he threw a stone at her window and then hid to see if she would come out. When she did, a frown on her face, he felt so ashamed of himself he avoided passing her house for the next month.

She had been on the early train to Jerusalem and here she was again, on the train back to Tel Aviv, a straw hat with a flower over her bobbed blonde hair. The carriage was crowded and hot, but he'd manage to squeeze through to get a window seat. She was already on the aisle. In the morning, she had sat down right next to him, fanning herself with a twice-folded copy of *Ha'aretz*. When she looked at him, he was afraid she knew that he had thrown the stone, but she just smiled and asked his name and age in a throaty Ashkenazi kind of voice and then said that her name was Alma and that it was very brave for a boy of eleven to take the train by himself and was someone meeting him at the station in Jerusalem? He told her that his name was Amos and that his father had sent him to bring his mother home before the war began.

Now, on the way back, she asked him where his mother was, but he didn't answer, just looked out the window and hoped she would take the newspaper out of her big leather bag. He saw her splotched reflection in the grimy pane of the window. She waited for an answer. The train rolled through Beit Safafa, Israel on the right, the Arabs on the left. It entered the forest. Instead of the newspaper, she took out three pencils and a large book. In the reflection, he saw her leaf slowly through scribbles until she came to a white page. She looked around at the other passengers, sitting in the seats and in the aisle and standing, and began to draw. He glanced out of the corner of his eye and saw faces, real ones and the ones on the page.

He was the oldest, that is the oldest of his mother's children, but not his father's. His father had had a wife before, who died. There were older brothers and sisters, but they were all married and none of them lived in the shantytown next to Holon's Samaritan settlement where a lot of Iraqis like them had been dumped when they came after independence. He'd been frying eggs and cutting cucumbers for supper for his three little brothers and sisters and hadn't had time, after doing his homework, to wash the floor or fold the laundry. His father came in, sweaty and tired from a long day at the stand in the market. He looked around the house, muttered something in Arabic and sighed. He patted the smaller children on the head, put his hand on Amos's shoulder, and said, this can't go on. Tomorrow you take the first train to Jerusalem and bring your mother home.

He watched her switch pencils and then quickly glanced at her page. She smiled. He looked out the window again.

That morning, he woke up the little ones half an hour earlier than usual, singing Nasser's waiting now for Rabin ai yai yai, Nasser's waiting now for Rabin, ai yai yai, just as his father was leaving for the market. He gave them all tea and sandwiches and walked them to school. Leaving them in the yard there with a few other early risers, he took the bus to the train station in Tel Aviv.

He told her none of this, but he had already said too much on the trip that morning. Family matters should stay inside the family, his father always told him. There should be no third parties.

He imagined his mother in the room with the small window where his grandmother lived. His grandmother, his mother insisted, could barely walk and needed someone to shop, clean and cook for her. So his mother took the train to Jerusalem once a month, which then became once a week, and now she had been there for three weeks straight and had sent word that she could not leave.

Because you are the oldest I can tell you this, I have to tell you this, his father had said the night before, after the little ones were asleep on their cots in the living room. It's my fault. I made a mistake. That is, I did not make a mistake. Not a mistake because I have you and your brother and sisters. But it was not fair to your mother, and I love her, but she … You see, my first wife died in Baghdad and left me with five children in school. My sister Katy helped at first, but then she told me that I had to remarry so that the children would have a mother and so I would have someone to keep the house. I had a store in the bazaar then, I sold fabric, you know about that, I did well. Preferably a young wife, Katy said, a strong and energetic one. She asked around. One day, she told me to come to her house that evening, she'd send her eldest to be with the children. Your mother was there with her mother. Her father had died two years before.

She was seventeen and very quiet. I was thirty-two and, what can I say? I still had an eye for a beautiful woman. No money in the family, Katy whispered to me, but that's not what you need. Her mother can't keep her. She followed my eye and smiled. You like her, she said. That's good.

You have a fine face, Alma suddenly said to him. He turned toward her in surprise, and she nodded, as if confirming her impression. He turned back to the window. She chose a different pencil and began to draw in the bottom right corner of her page, below her sketch of the crowd around them. His face, he saw through the soot and dust on the window.

He stared out, knowing that she was looking at him, waiting patiently. He traced out a head—a circle, dots for eyes, half-hearts for ears, in the dust on the pane.

Would you like a pencil and paper?

He shrugged.

His father told him that his young new wife did everything that was expected of her. She cleaned and cooked and bore him children. When, that terrible night, they had to pack up what little they could, abandon business and home, and set off for Israel, she did not scream or weep or curse like other women. Efficiently, quietly, intensely, she chose the essentials, dressed the children, and stood by the door.

I was terribly fond of her, but did not tell her that, his father said. It was all so clear and obvious then, for a girl to marry so young, for an orphan to be grateful that an older man put a roof over her head and provided for her. Only after they arrived, when they lived first in a tent in the mud on this very spot in the sands, then when he built the house and, to feed them all, he had to work as a hawker selling bananas in the market, did he start to realize that she was unhappy. Her mother was far off, in Jerusalem, and he thought it was that. He suggested the trips. She nodded, and went.

I understand her, his father said. I have a heart. But we need her, don't we? Who knows if we won't have to pack up and leave again soon, for some other country? It all falls on you, with me at work. She has responsibilities, after all. She is your mother. You must bring her back.

Alma reached out and touched a soft white cotton handkerchief to his cheek.

That morning, from the train station in Jerusalem, he had taken the bus to Mahaneh Yehuda. There he walked between the hawkers of bananas, cucumbers, melons, all tall, short, fat, thin copies of his father. Then through the Iraqi market to the courtyard where men with moustaches smoked and played backgammon. As he was about to step into the alley on the far side, he stopped. A woman was singing. He realized, suddenly, that he had never heard his mother sing before. There were no words, her voice was like a violin's, but he knew the Arabic words to the song. *Ruhi tilfat*, my soul is weary. He saw his mother on her hands and knees, scrubbing the stoop in front of his grandmother's door, her back to him. He did not even stop to think. He turned around and returned to the bus stop.

The woman from Rassco held up her sketchbook and turned it toward him. He glanced and saw the crowd, and he saw his face at the bottom of the page. It was his face not as he'd seen it in the window, but as it felt inside.

It is so easy to be by oneself among so many people, she said.

She waited.

What will your father say?

He shrugged.

Would it help if I come with you?

He turned to her, angry. He won't beat me, if that's what you think. There's nothing you can do.

Her eyes were soft. I could teach you to draw.

He looked at the page open before her.

Would it help if I come with you? Or should we each go home alone? She waited for him.

He wept, like the boy in her sketchbook, and then he nodded. He did not know to what, or why.

Piano Lesson

I am impressed. You play like a Jew, Felix. What I mean is that you have Johann Sebastian Bach in your heart as well as in your fingertips. Please don't tell your mother I said this. She'd be upset to hear that she hasn't succeeded in bleaching Israel out of you. How mortified she would be if, in the middle of an intellectual evening here in this very parlor, von Humboldt were to apply his magnifying glass to you and say: "Aha! A fine specimen of Mendelssohnius Judaeas!"

What's that? Speak up! And please do not call me Aunt Sara. Approximating family relationships is like slurring a *gruppetto*. I am and will always be your Great Aunt Sara. If you wish, you may, in the grand company that gathers so frequently in this room, be even more precise and refer to me as "Great Aunt Sara Itzig Levy." And you may add, if asked, "Yes, the daughter of Daniel Itzig and Miriam Wulff, intimates of the illustrious philosopher Moses Mendelssohn, she who studied keyboard with Friedmann Bach, Johann Sebastian's oldest son, and who has kept the sweet music of the elder Bach alive in her salon through decades of public indifference." That will do.

And wipe that smirk off your face. There is nothing more unattractive than the smirk of a seventeen-year-old boy.

Oh, yes, at your age, you know it all. Music is universal. How can the notes emerging from a pianoforte be Jewish, you ask? Felix, you know nothing at all. Remember that I told you this today, in Berlin, in July 1826, because some years from now, you will realize how true it was of you when you were young.

Listen to me. And stop cracking your knuckles. You will ruin your joints. This piece you have played so beautifully for me this morning, the Partita No. 5 in G Major, can only be played properly, in our *falscherleuchtung* age, this time of false enlightenment, by a person of Jewish sensibility. Please do not interrupt me. At your age, you are to listen to your elders first. After you listen, you may disagree, you may do whatever you want. But first you must listen.

Sebastian Bach was a devout Lutheran, true, but he wrote Jewish music. I do not say this simply to embellish the repute of my ancestral people. The nation Israel needs no trills. I say this after long years of study and performance of Bach's music, during which I have come to know this remarkable man. Better, I hazard to say, than his own sons did.

What is Jewish about the music? To see that, you have to know music. Which, of course, you know. You also have to know what Judaism is. Which, thanks to my niece, you do not. This is scandalous. The grandson of the great Moses Mendelssohn knows nothing of his own people's special relationship with God. Or I should say, he knows what every self-satisfied Prussian burgher knows, which is that the God of the Old Testament is harsh and vindictive and that his erstwhile people have hopelessly lost their way in a tangle of laws and observances in which the King of Heaven himself long ago lost interest.

When you've had enough of tugging at those curls of yours you might play movement three, the Courante, once more. It's your favorite? I am not surprised. It's so jumpy and exuberant that I think Bach must have been feeling seventeen when he wrote it. No, he was in his forties. But he was as exuberant as a young man.

Not so fast. Pay attention to what you are doing here. In these measures. Seven through nine. Do you hear what you have done? That hint of emphasis here, and again here? Now isn't that Jewish?

You're asking yourself, what does this crazy old lady want of me? Oh yes, I see it in your eyes. Don't deny it. Great aunts know. Now you've got me smirking as well.

Look. How many measures in this first section? Yes, thirty-two. And how many phrases. Four, very good. How many measures per phrase?

Come now. Four into thirty-two. Eight. Eight measures per phrase? Isn't that what the rules require? Bach, after all, is baroque. Baroque means very strict rules. Everything is very regular, very predictable. That's what everyone says. That's why they don't want to listen to this music. Why listen to something so banal when you can listen to Ludwig Beethoven put his diarrhea into demisemiquavers? Excuse me. But you know what I mean. If there are thirty-two measures and four phrases, there must be eight measures in each phrase. So unexciting.

So where does the first phrase end? Look at the chords.

Very good. On this G. The first note of the ninth measure. Not the last note of the eighth measure, but that's close enough, don't you think?

So your right hand should immediate pick up the melody of the second phrase after that G.

So what is your right hand doing at that point? Don't you see? It started the new melodic phrase a measure before. E-F-D-A-D-F-D, the motif repeated here in measure ten but one note down, D-F-C-G-C-E-C.

So is Bach obeying the rules or breaking them?

Some day you might read your grandfather's books. If you can find them, because I understand that your mother and father have made your house *Judenrein* and that one cannot find anything prior to the Gospels on the shelves here. But perhaps they have copies hidden away in some secret corner. If so, you will find that Moses our teacher received two types of laws from our Creator. There is the written law and the oral law. The written law is what you see in the Five Books of Moses and the Oral Law is the supplementary material and interpretations handed down by our Sages. In each generation, the Sages are authorized—indeed required—to understand the law in accordance with the needs of the moment and to rule accordingly. No, this is not antinomianism. The law is fundamental. But the law is not a single note that never changes. It is a melodic line that flows from the tonic and returns to it inexorably in the end.

If Bach were to have taken his thirty-two-measure "A" section and divided it neatly into four eight-measure phrases, he would have been meek and law-abiding and boring. But our lives are not boring, or at least they should not be if we truly experience God, if we love those close to us, if we marvel at the world around us. All these things were created and are maintained by divine and natural law, but none of them are dull.

Nowadays, in this time when people think they are so modern, composers simply cast off all discipline and write what is in their hearts, they say, although I believe it often comes from their colons. They write overtures and fantasias and serenades and meditations but they, like your mother and father, take the easy way out. What emerges is bland, amorphous, unworthy of music's high calling.

I first performed this Partita at Rahel Varnhagen's salon, I believe it was some time in the 1790s when the world was aflame. In preparing the piece for a public concert, I initially had difficulty with the Courante. Friedmann Bach had taught me to stress phrase boundaries, but here I could not see where the stress should go. I consulted with him and he was rather dismissive: "The old man couldn't make up his mind," he said.

I kept working on the piece and the morning prior to the performance, I had my epiphany. Here, let me play it for you.

So where is the stress? Yes, here. And here too. At the end of the melodic line. And at the end of the harmonic progression. Which do not coincide.

You see, the underlying harmonics here are the Torah, the Written Law. And the melody playing above it is the Oral Law. The melody would be hollow, meaningless without the underlying harmony, and the underlying harmony would be incomplete and useless without the melody above it.

The simple-minded might think that the two laws should coincide. What good is a God if His message is not clear?

Yet it is the lack of clarity, the occasional dissonance, the unsynchronized phrases that move us forward, that propel us toward the final resolution. And that final tonic itself sends us off into new melodic and harmonic firmaments, from which we again return to our G major chord. One idea begins before the previous idea has been completed. As when you interrupt your Great Aunt Sara.

Well, I'm glad that excites you. Because I heard the elision of those phrases in your fingers when you played the piece through for me. Oh, yes, I did. That is why I said you play like a Jew. I seldom need to correct great-nephew Felix's technique. But I do need to help him understand why he plays as he does.

What's that? Why can't you enunciate? Sebastian Bach is what? "Awesome?" Is that how you young people speak today? Fine, let him be "awesome." Oh yes, I've got a whole library of scores and parts that you can study. Just come and pay your great aunt a visit. Remind me to show you the *Matthew Passion*. It is such wonderfully *Jewish* music!

Hooligan Oil

Hooligan oil? Did you say hooligan oil? I'm so sorry, I was deep into this letter from my sister back east, I didn't even hear you come into the store. It's so quiet this time of day, in the early afternoon, sometimes I just close up and go for a walk.

Alaska's spring is so beautiful this year, the lupines are blooming early and it's simply glorious. I always tell my girls, Sarah, Minnie, I say, there is so much to look at in this world, I mean irises the color of the purple of Sidon. Turn your gaze on them, not on Harry and Joe, the ships' boys on the passenger steamer from Dyea. You might notice that the irises, unlike Harry and Joe, don't have pimples. Max, Simon, I say, don't walk with your eyes on the ground, look around you, see what an Eden God has given you here in Skagway.

Now let me see, hooligan oil, not many people ask for that any more, but you know that they used to call it "liquid gold." It made the natives' fortune, before the solid stuff was discovered. I know some women who say it prevents wrinkles, but others can't stand the smell. Once Max, he is only twelve but a true rascal, got hold of a bunch of those fish, hung them from the rafters in his and Simon's bedroom, and lit the tails. Nearly burned the house down! He said that he wanted to see if what the old-timers said was true, that you could use the fish as candles. You want to be scientists, I'll send you to Harvard, I said. No experiments at home. But better they should study medicine. It's one profession where we people can make our mark, where we get some respect.

No need to say it in such a low voice. Nothing to be ashamed of. Yes, Jews. Everyone in Skagway knows exactly who I am. Except these people, look at this letter, from the Women's Christian Temperance Union of Sitka, who want me to ban drink from Skagway. But we Jews are brought up to drink responsibly, a glass of wine every Friday night and Saturday morning. But they are almost right about something else, those dry women in Sitka—women's suffrage. I replied to them this morning, see, the letter here is ready for mailing, and I told them that I would be most pleased to join their crusade to grant women the vote, on one condition—that we also take the vote away from men. Why? Just go out and talk to the first five of them you run into on the street and you'll see.

Hey, why are you taking that letter? I have to mail it! You're what? The new postmaster? But you weren't supposed to arrive until next Monday! Well, I am pleased to make your acquaintance. Mr. Baxter, your predecessor, would see me on the street and call out to everyone around, Here's my best customer! Without Peppy Samuels the US mails would have no reason to come to Skagway!

Yes, it's very sad about Mr. Baxter, but livers will do that to you if you drink as much whiskey as he did. I hope the Portland sun will offer him some solace.

And your name? Mr. Harold Fein? Why, that's a Jewish name! And is the hooligan oil for Mrs. Fein? I mean, I can't imagine that she needs any, you look barely thirty, so she must be quite young and pretty.

There is no Mrs. Fein?

Well, you are number seven, if you count my children, which you should. Number six is Aloysius Bloch, who gave up prospecting last winter and founded *The Daily Alaskan*. I don't count Mamie Schwarzkopf, whom you'll hear called Imogene Astor because that's what she goes by, but I know exactly who she is. But you'll agree with me that it's for the best of all concerned that a proprietress of a house of ill repute not be associated with our ancient heritage. But I give credit where credit is due—it is the *largest* and *cleanest* of the many such establishments in Skagway—it's our business sense and hygiene, no sir, you can't take that away from us. My Max is confined to his room today because I caught him lurking just a little too close to Mamie's place yesterday evening. "Oh, Ma," he said, "I just felt like my racial instincts were drawing me toward a fellow Jew!" "I'll mention that in my next letter to Herr Doktor Herzl," I said. "I'm sure he will agree with me that the instincts in question were not racial at all. We have a reputation to keep up in Skagway." He's a good boy, they are all good children, but try bringing them up wholesome and pure in such a place. Maybe I should have sent them away to school a long time ago. But without them, what do I have here? My Morris ...

Thank you, I'm so sorry, look, I smudged your handkerchief. I so seldom lose control like this anymore. I'm keeping you. I must find you that hooligan oil. In this drawer, yes, I remember. No, it's the only size we have, but it doesn't spoil. Is there anything else? You aren't in a hurry? Show you around town? Well, I would be delighted. My keys are right here. But let me just put this letter in my bag. From my maiden sister Lillian. Feel how thick the envelope is even though she writes on fine onionskin stationery.

She is already on the Northern Pacific, chugging her way to Seattle and thence by steamer to here. She says she misses the children, but I know how to read between the lines of her delicate ladylike penmanship. She is coming at the behest of my parents, Dr. Elias and Mrs. Harriet Samuels, to take me home to Philadelphia.

Lillian was always the obedient one. Look where it got her. Papa and Mama are strict German types who tried to plan our lives out to the last detail. In the end, one daughter flew the coop and the other never left home.

They had very specific ideas about my life. I also had very specific ideas, but they were different from theirs. They wanted me to be a prim and proper lady, to marry up, to run a genteel bourgeois household. I wanted to dance, to travel, to create, to have adventures. After graduating, I wanted to go to Paris, but they had already planned a wedding. They just forgot to tell me about it. I was to move to Charleston as the wife of a forty-year old textile exporter named Blaustein who was twice the size of President Cleveland. I screamed, I cried, I even packed my suitcase to run off to New York by myself, but Lillian saw and told Papa. He locked me in my room. I thought I would die.

But they didn't shutter the windows, and I saw Morris bicycling down the street with a parcel balanced between his handlebars. He was in his shirtsleeves and had his cap cocked to one side and was whistling loudly. He stopped by our house, slow and easy so as not to drop the package, and then I lost sight of him. Then I heard the bell ring and our Betsy's voice saying something and the door closing.

When Betsy brought me my lunch, I waited until she was almost out the door and asked what had been delivered. She said some tools the gardener needed to fix the shed in the yard. I asked who delivered it and she said a young man named Morris from Gimbels who had joked with her and made her blush.

That evening at dinner, I told Mama and Papa that I had thought the matter over and now believed that Mr. Blaustein would make an excellent husband, and that I wanted to proceed with the engagement. But I really must have some new things, I told them, and suggested that Mama and I make a trip to Gimbels the next day.

Mama was only too happy to take me there, though when we arrived she kept complaining that I was straining and staring instead of paying attention to the seamstress who was pinning the dress we had chosen. Finally, in desperation, I asked the saleswoman where the facilities might be, and once Mama was out of sight I asked at the haberdashery desk where the delivery boys could be found and, following his directions, I found myself in a corridor that smelled of sawdust, and knocked on a door to a back room.

Well, God must have been on my side because the delivery boy who opened the door was Morris, Morris Skolnik, as I soon found out. He was somewhat surprised to see a young woman at the door inquiring into what he might be doing that evening, but as soon as he understood my drift, a wide, beautiful smile broke out all over his face. And, as the stories go, that evening he cast pebbles at my window. I told Mama that I really must get some air and that Betsy (who was surprised no end) would be going for a short walk with me. We walked down the street to Fairmount Park as I swore Betsy to secrecy and there Morris was waiting for me.

Well, once I'd held Morris's hand on a park bench, there was no way I was going to Charleston. Morris was everything Mr. Blaustein could never be—young, funny, determined to make something of himself. Mama wept and Papa bellowed. They told me I was dooming myself to a life of poverty by marrying a delivery boy. But in the meantime, Morris was making a fine impression on the Philadelphia Gimbel, who promoted him to stockroom clerk and then, just three months later, to chief of inventory. Soon he was practically running the store! He knew how to get and keep customers, how to manage his stock and treat staff well, and everyone at Bnai Abraham started congratulating Mama about that talented young businessman soon to be her son-in-law, who was so polite, even if he did speak Yiddish.

Here, just let me lock the door. Now you must excuse me, but I have a rather personal question to ask you. You don't mind? Good. Will you marry me?

Did I shock you with my proposal? I know that etiquette requires that I wait for you to ask. Women are only supposed to cast modest glances and drop hints that they would be delighted to receive a proposal. But most men are such dimwits that the hints go right by them and so single-minded that the glances are not seen as modest. Furthermore, I can't wait. Lillian will be here in two weeks at the most.

That's the boarding house run by Mrs. Pullen, who can be a little too much. Many of the bachelors eat their dinners there, but she's been known to serve horse and bear, so you are always welcome to share what we have. I can't claim that the rabbi who married me would eat my food, but we live in unusual circumstances and try to keep the spirit, if not the letter, of the law. Over there? The tracks? That's the train to nowhere, that's what I call it. Crazy man with wads of money came over from England to build a train that goes over White Pass into gold territory. Have you ever seen a train climb straight up into the air? That's what it's going to have to do. And for what? They'll soon find gold somewhere else, somewhere where you don't need to lug all your gear up a mountain in the freezing snow, and as soon as they do, no one will come to Skagway anymore. No, I'm not worried. The whores and drunks will leave, but there is great potential here. Did I mention that I am the chairwoman of the Skagway Music and Culture Society? We are holding our first program a week from Monday, Aloysius will play Brahms on the piano, and Sarah, Minnie, and two of their friends will perform an original ballet that I have choreographed, expressing the awful beauty of the Alaskan coast. I danced when I was at Smith and I was quite good. I have been in correspondence with Mrs. Jeannette Thurber, the founder of the National Conservatory of Music of America in New York City. I'm sure you have heard of her. She is a great patron of the arts, and I have impressed on her the vital importance of bringing high culture to the American frontier. I believe that she may provide some funding for our little project.

Here, we've reached the docks and there's a nice breeze. Let's sit here on this wall and look at the ocean.

How was life with my Morris? It was all I could ask for. I didn't mind living in a smaller house and I certainly didn't mind it that I was not a *hausfrau*. I took a bookkeeping course and Morris convinced Gimbel to give me a job in the back office, doing the accounts. I showed I was no less diligent than Morris, and soon I was promoted as well. I worked straight through my pregnancies, no confinement for me. First Sarah came, then Minnie, then Max, then finally Simon. Mama was scandalized that I worked every day, but on the other hand she and Betsy were quite happy to have the children.

Morris and I were successes, but we saw where we were heading—to the same kind of life my parents led. We both had an itch.

We knew there was more to life than a donor's plaque on the wall of Bnai Abraham. We talked, on breaks in the back office, about moving the family out west, maybe to San Francisco, or perhaps even to Hong Kong.

Then one day, on my way back from the Post Office, I stopped in Leary's Book Store, next to Gimbels, one of my favorite places. I'd ordered a copy of Mr. Wells' new novel and went to pick it up. Julius, the sales clerk, presented me with two books, not one. When I said there had been a mistake, he said that, no, the boss had specifically said that I should be given the second volume as well, and that I should be informed that he would be extremely displeased if I did not purchase and read it.

On the cover was a log cabin, topped by a strange animal totem, in a gray landscape. Two small figures stood by the cabin, with their backs to the reader. The title was *Alaska: Its Southern Coast and the Sitkan Archipelago* and the author was Mrs. Eliza Ruhamah Scidmore. I'd never heard of her, but her middle name caught my eye. Scidmore was obviously not a Jewish name, but Ruhama, I remembered from my childhood lessons, means "comfort," and, oddly, that stormy, dreary picture comforted me—it promised a world different from my own. I began reading that night. Mrs. Scidmore turned out to be a woman of adventure, the kind of woman I'd always longed to be. Two days later, I finished it and gave it to Morris. Halfway through, in the back office, he clapped the book shut and looked me in the eye. "Alaska," he said. "Good things are going to happen there."

Alaska was the new frontier, a place where a man could start from scratch and, just like the Gimbel brothers, turn a family store into an empire.

He turned serious. "Of course, you'll be very far from your Mama and Papa."

"Oh, no!" I said in mock horror. "When can we leave?"

Well, for the next three months, Morris collected all the information he could about Alaska, focusing on where the best location for Skolnik's Dry Goods would be. He soon settled on Skagway, which he reasoned was a small town on its way to greatness. The Canadians' attempts to lay claim to the area meant that the army and navy would have to ratchet up their presence. That meant visiting ships and an army garrison that needed to be provisioned. There were already established shipping lines from San Francisco, Portland, and Seattle, so stocking the store would be no problem. Morris was convinced that, as soon as the border dispute was settled, travelers like Mrs. Scidmore would be coming by, first more adventurous ones and then less and then, who knows, whole families!

In April 1895, Morris asked for a year's leave from Gimbels and boarded the Pennsylvania Railroad on his way to San Francisco. Mama was, of course, scandalized, and Papa tried to get me dismissed so that I could be a proper mother to my children. But I needed the income and loved the work. From San Francisco Morris wrote enthusiastic but judicious letters about the contacts he made with suppliers. He was very careful, had his feet on the ground, didn't sign anything without checking every angle. Then in early June, he took a steamer to Alaska and reached Skagway later that month with his initial inventory. He rented the store, the same building you found me in, hired some idle men to help him redo it, and put out his shutter at the beginning of August.

Was it good business sense or providence? At the end of the month, a bedraggled prospecting party came down the pass and announced they'd discovered gold on Rabbit Creek. Rabbit Creek was 600 miles away in the Klondike, but to get there you had to go through Skagway. Suddenly there was money in the territory, and as word spread men started moving in.

Morris wired me: "More work than I can handle. Pack up things and children. Come immediately."

Mama screamed. Papa disowned me. Gimbels offered me a raise and promised to make Morris a senior manager if he would just come back. "We're going to live with Indians!" Max told a shocked Rabbi Gottlieb at Sunday school. "And see whales!" Simon chortled.

Traveling cross-country with four small children—I could write a book about that. Max still hasn't forgiven me for grabbing the rifle out of his hands just when he'd taken aim at a bison.

The sea leg of our trip was much easier for me. We set sail on a boatful of whores, and they went wild over the children, especially over Simon, who at four years old was at the height of his impish stage. At first I tried to keep them away, but I quickly learned that these women of the night were just like other people. Some were truly immoral—lazy, rude, slovenly, and selfish—but others were of high intellect and refinement. One, with the interesting name of Aspen, had a trunkload of books and introduced me to a writer who had thus far evaded my attention, Mr. Henry James. She lent me his novel, *Portrait of a Lady*, and I was astounded to see an American writer who could get so intimately into the minds of his women characters. Aspen and I often call on each other to share books and thoughts. You might not believe this, but she pays dues to the Women's Christian Temperance Union and, in her professional contacts with men, seeks to wean them from the bottle. She is able to offer them certain attractive alternatives.

To make a long story short, we landed in Skagway, Morris installed us in a house, acquainted me with the business and, two weeks after our arrival, contracted a strange and fierce fever. Two days later, he was dead.

I don't want to watch the waves anymore. Would you mind walking me back to the store? Thank you so very much.

I like the way you laughed, back in the store. The laugh itself and the fact that it is a joyful laugh, one full of fun, not of derision or of shock. Morris laughed like that. It makes me feel young again.

After Morris passed on, Mama and Papa wired me five hundred dollars and told me to come home immediately. I wired it back to them and said, *Thank you, I have a business to manage, one with great potential.* And business has been flourishing. I have put aside a considerable nest egg, enough to send the children to good schools when they come of age. And I'm not a fool like so many of the prospectors here, who hand their money over to swindlers and card sharks or spend it on drink and women.

But Mama and Papa have not given up. They have sent Lillian to fetch me back. They cannot accept that a woman can fend for herself. They cannot bear to have their grandchildren growing up among gentiles, gamblers, and harlots.

That's why I need to have a husband, a Jewish one, in hand when Lillian arrives. If I do, she'll have nothing to say. She can't break the bond of holy matrimony, can she? And a postmaster is even better than a newspaper editor for respectability.

This is where you are staying? At Mrs. Pullen's? Oh, my! Aren't boarding houses sad? I'm sure you'd prefer to live with a family and hear the pitter-patter of children rather than the groans and sighs of other lonely men. Whatever you do, don't eat her meat.

How nice that you came into the store and suggested this walk! Do you have your hooligan oil? Good. I'm not yet at an age where I need to worry so much about wrinkles that I need to put up with the smell. You must be tired. Take a nap. Consider my offer. I'll be back at the store, catching up on my correspondence. I must convey to Dr. Herzl my plan to colonize the Alaskan panhandle with Hungarian Jews. And Mrs. Thurber has not replied to my latest letter and I must send her a reminder. So I'll have many letters to send by the end of the day. If you don't come to get them, I'll drop them off at the post office tomorrow morning.

Cloudburst

The man grunts into a chair at the table next to me at Aroma Sokolov. The hair on his fleshy overworked fingers is thicker than the hair on his head. A tan sweater, a size too tight for him, outlines his bulging belly. His eyes and nose are both watery from the droplets of exhaust that shiver in the winter morning air in Holon. He unfolds his free copy of *Yisra'el Hayom* and, in response to a query from a young man standing at the counter, holds up two of those thick fingers. He flips the paper to look at the forecast, shakes his head, and settles back in his chair.

"Dry January, right?" he says to me. "But then each year is drier than the last."

I nod and give him a smile with which I try to say, "You know it!" but also, "I'm kind of busy so leave me alone."

"But that cloudburst last night? Did you catch it? At two in the morning?"

When I don't respond, he nods in the direction of the counter. "That's my son, Niv. He's getting married next week."

"Mazal tov." No exclamation point.

"He's a good kid. Great girl, too." Niv, drumming a riff on the counter while he waits, has a runner's build and a frazzle of rusty hair.

"Looks it." I keep my eyes on my laptop screen.

"Love, you know." He laughs. "It changes everything."

I ignore him, and he gives up and returns to the newspaper. "Niv!" says a loudspeaker voice. A moment later, the son places a tray on the table next to me and sits down. He carefully, respectfully lifts a glass mug of kafeh hafukh from the bright orange tray and puts it in front of his father, followed by a small plate bearing a jelly donut and two tiny metal jugs of extra hot milk, which he nudges gently toward his father's mug. Tearing a packet of sugar with his teeth, he sweetens his own hafukh, which remains on the tray. From a pants pocket, he draws an iPhone and positions it next to the coffee. The two of them sip silently, long enough for me to forget they are there.

"Did you catch that cloudburst at two?" the father says.

Niv glances outside and shakes his head. "No, but I saw it was wet this morning."

"It reminded me of when I was on maneuvers in the paratroopers in '75. Out in the desert near Nebi Musa."

The son looks quizzically at his father, who hesitates, as if ready to check himself and return to silence. "I'd just met your mother. We weren't really, like, romantic yet, but I knew that was coming." He spoons foam off his coffee and shakes his head. "It's too bad ..." He cuts his thought off in the middle, squeezes the mug hard, and goes on.

"We were practicing our company's act for the battalion exercise later in the week. We were supposed to capture the Marsaba monastery. Did you guys do that? It's a bitch. Of course, you can't do live fire on a monastery, it would be an international incident, so you do it a couple hills over, pretend-like. That's what we would do in the battalion exercise, but Jabbo, our company commander—he was a real dick—decided we should do a dry assault on the monastery, and there we were all afternoon—and you know down there by the Dead Sea, it can get hot as hell, even in the winter— and we were running like idiots up the side of the mountain shouting 'Fire! Fire!' with the monks staring at us and probably taking notes about our tactics to send to the Arabs."

Niv looks straight into his father's eyes, but the man averts his gaze.

"So the sun set behind the mountains above us and that freezing desert evening wind began blowing, chilling the sweat on our fatigues and turning them into air conditioners, if you know what I mean."

Niv nods.

"And we're looking up, waiting for the stars to come out, and you know down there how they blaze, you see stars that no one in Holon knows exist, and no stars come out. And then my buddy Guy wipes something out of his eye and we realize there aren't any stars because black clouds have blown in and out of the black, with no warning, the hillside lights up in a huge flash and there's an explosion like nothing we had in our arsenal. There's no air, it's all water, like a river coming down from the sky, and in five seconds, we and our gear are totally drenched. And we're freezing, shivering like someone pushed us into a refrigerator, but also happy because we know that there's no way we can keep exercising in this weather, we'll all get pneumonia, and probably a flash flood is already thundering down the wadi from Jerusalem, But Jabbo calls out, 'One more time, guys! This is a cloudburst, it'll be over in five minutes!' He runs along our line, bopping us on our helmets and kicking our bottoms, he has us running up the mountain, shouting, 'Fire! Fire!' even though we're sinking in the mud, and the only difference is that the monks, who are ten times smarter than we are, have gone inside where it's dry."

Niv's cell phone vibrates. He glances at it and a smile plays over his face as he picks it up. "Hedvi," he says, and the way he says it make me think about how much meaning two syllables can bear. He listens for a few seconds and says "I'm having coffee with my Dad. I'll call back when I'm done?" He listens, nods, and puts the phone down.

"She's ok?" the father asks.

"She forgot to turn the heat off before she went out," Niv says. "I'll go by after I take you home."

The Dad wipes donut jelly from his face. He looks into his coffee. Sips some. Looks some more. The son fidgets.

"So you were soaking wet. And getting pneumonia."

"Right, right," the father says. "So finally Jabbo is convinced we can conquer any monastery in any weather and tells us to pack up. Some cloudburst, it's still coming down, and we have three kilometers to walk back to camp. With all the gear on our backs, it takes us half an hour to get there."

"Wow," Niv says.

"It was different then. We slept in pup tents. We each got half a tent, just a piece of oilcloth, and poles, and you teamed up with a buddy and built a pup tent. Well, you remember meeting Guy. He was just as huge then as now. So he took up pretty much the whole tent, and I had to squeeze in next to him. Of course, the tent was soaked, and everything was mud, even though camp was on top of a hill, it was all washed out, but you know that a soldier can sleep anywhere, in any situation, all he wants to do is sleep, so we get to our tent and Guy crawls in, and before I can even take my vest off, he's snoring. I can't see a thing, of course, so I take out my flashlight, it's a miracle, the rain hasn't shorted it out, and I shine it in and, well, you know how when you wet a sponge, it soaks up all the water and doubles its size? Well, Guy was like a sponge. I look in and he's pressing up against the sides of the tent on all sides and there's not a crevice for me to squeeze into.

"And then I think, Why should I even try, and I don't know how it suddenly came to me, I wasn't any more a man to pray then than I am now, but I said to myself, Hey, I bet the synagogue tent is dry, the religious guys must have made sure that their Torah wouldn't get wet, so I trudge over there and look inside and it's empty and there are a few rows of wooden benches and even wooden pallets on the floor and the benches are dry. And there's a blanket covering the table they read from, and another on another table, and four more stacked in a corner, and that's better than my waterlogged sleeping bag, so I push three of the benches together and put down a blanket and take off all my clothes, every last stitch, and dry myself with one blanket, and cover myself with the others, and, let me tell you, I've never slept better. And when I got woken up in the morning by the religious guys coming to pray, the sun was out and ravens were caw- ing and Jabbo was shouting, and I was dry and warm, but my back was so sore I could barely move. Also, I was naked. They called the medic, who examined me as they were swaying and chanting, and he said I needed to rest, and I ended up spending the whole day sleeping in the infirmary and dreaming about your mother and it was maybe the best day of my life up until then."

The father looks at his son as if expecting a response, but not knowing what response he expects, he waits.

"It's a good story," the son says, glancing at his phone.

"I'm telling you this," the father says, "because ..." but then his voice fades. He pours the warm milk from the two metal jugs into his coffee and drains the mug. "Because you are getting married."

The son gives him a questioning look and the telephone vibrates once again. He tells the phone, "We're just finishing. I'm already on my way." And to his father: "I need to get going. I'll take you home. I'll just go to the bathroom, and I'll be right back."

"And when I woke up at two in the morning last night," the father says, but now with his son gone, he's speaking directly to me, "alone in bed, I got up and went to the bathroom and then walked into the living room. I looked out the window and the rain began coming down, just like that, a huge storm, like from the beginning of the world, and I stood there watching it streak under the streetlights for maybe five or six minutes until it ended just as suddenly as it began. 'Oh, a cloudburst,' I said to myself, and smiled, and I remembered that day, lying in the infirmary and dreaming about the rest of my life ..."

The son is back. "What were you saying, Dad?"

The father glances at me. He shakes his head. "It's too bad you missed it. The cloudburst. It was like love."

Inta Omri

Ilana elbows me and eyes the couple sitting to our left in the Hirsch Theater. I am shaken out of the reverie brought on by Um Kulthum's hit song "*Raq al-Habib*," "The Servitude of Love." Against the background of the Tarshiha Orchestra, the woman to my left is tapping out a text message on her Android as she whispers to her husband, who has a large knitted blue-and-white kipah on his head.

"Hadas," she says, apparently in response to his question.

"Did you tell her?" he asks.

"Doing it right now," she nods.

I catch her eye and put a finger to my lips. I also point to the phone, as if to say that the glow is distracting me. She shrugs and mutters, "Almost done."

"Did she say anything about Ya'akov? Why he didn't come home?"

The young woman who is standing in for the late great Egyptian chanteuse finishes the song with a flourish, and the audience cheers. Nasim Dawkar, the concertmaster and conductor, calls a different member of the chorus up to the solo microphone to sing another song composed by Muhammad al-Qasabgi, to whose works the night's concert is dedicated. The woman at the mike, plump and heavily made up, launches into an Um Kulthum favorite, "*Inta 'Omri*," "You are My Life." Ilana smiles and mouths the words silently—it's a song her mother used to sing to her and which Ilana sings to our own children.

Over the years, I've come to appreciate Arab music. Now I know why at first it sounded like annoying noise—it's based on an entirely different scale from Western music, one with notes, microtones, between the notes we know, a music of unisons rather than harmonies, where structure and meaning are provided by repeating rhythmic and melodic motives rather than harmonic progressions. The Tarshiha Orchestra is composed mostly of stringed instruments—eight violins, a cello and double bass, an oud, a zither, and percussion, with a single ney flute as the only wind.

My neighbor's phone beeps. She reads, and hisses at her husband: "She can't believe it."

"Believe what?" says the husband in an undertone that was barely under.

"That he's sitting just two rows in front of us."

"Are you sure it's him?"

"I mean, I took his picture and sent it to Ze'ev, and Ze'ev says bingo!"

"Excuse me," I say very quietly, "but we came here to listen to the music."

"Oh, so did we!" says the husband, leaning over his wife. "She's really great, isn't she?" And he begins clapping the rhythm with much of the rest of the audience.

Um Kulthum of Tarshiha launches into an extended *gruppetto* that rises and falls and rises and falls again like a tsunami of adoration for the light of her life. The audience goes wild. A man two rows in front of us jumps to his feet, hooting and applauding.

I feel a hand on my wrist. It's the woman next to me. She gives me a quick glance out of the corner of her eye as if commanding me to follow her gaze to the applauding man.

"That's him," she says. "Do you know what he did to my daughter-in-law?"

"Tell her you don't care what anyone did to her daughter-in-law," Ilana whispers angrily in my right ear.

But my neighbor is gripping my wrist and my not-so-subtle efforts to wriggle free makes no impression on her.

"*Dou' ma-aya el hob, Dou' haba bei haba,*" the plump woman sings, clasping her fingers together and closing her eyes. "Taste love with me, taste a bit at a time, from my tender heart."

"My daughter-in-law works at VAT," the woman stage-whispers at me.

"The tax men. Big office building in Givat Sha'ul," the man says proudly. "Not a secretary, no, she's an accountant. Studied at Hebrew U."

"She's Tunisian."

"Her family," the man corrects. "Dark and beautiful, that's what our son Ya'akov likes."

"We're Iraqis," the woman reassures me.

"No way," Ilana, who is Iraqi, hisses in my other ear. "Iraqis would be too cultured to chat in the middle of a concert. Obviously Kurds."

"Well, northern Iraq," the woman says defensively.

"But Iraq," her husband insists.

"Anyway, Hadas, that's my daughter-in-law, she was born on Sukkot so they called her Hadas, she has to take a file up to the collection office two floors above."

"She works on the tenth floor," the man interjects.

"*Ya aghla min ahlmi,*" sings the distant lover from the Galilee, "Oh, more beautiful than my dreams, take me to your gentleness, take me from my life to far away."

"So she gets on the elevator," the woman says. "And who's there but this young Arab guy who cleans the bathrooms."

"I think he's sort of a handyman. I don't think he cleans the bathrooms," her husband adds. "That's what Hadas said, handyman."

"She told me he cleans the bathrooms," the woman insists. "Anyway, none of the girls in the office like him. They say he's strange, that he always stands too close, tries to talk to them, you know what I mean? You can tell when someone is just a little bit off."

"It's a big elevator," the man says. He places a set of calloused fingers on top of his wife's hand, which has, in the meantime, worked its way up to my forearm.

"It's a big elevator, but where does he stand? Not a centimeter between him and her!" Her eyes open wide. "Imagine! And she's a married woman, a mother! And he starts singing to her!"

"*Inta 'omri, illi ibtada b'nurak sabahuh,*" the deep alto sings, lilting around a single note, a bit up, a bit down, and then returning. "You are my life, the dawn begins with your light!"

"She sort of pushes him away and he gets angry, curses her. Well, Hadas is scared stiff. She gets off on floor twelve and calls me right away."

"See, our son, Ya'akov, is in Hong Kong on business," the man explains.

"He sells apps," the woman says. "Apps and links."

"Does very well," the man brags. "Travels all over the world. Weeks at a time." Then he adds: "Hadas gets lonely sometimes."

"No, she doesn't," his wife snaps.

"She told me."

"She's happy to have Ya'akov. What more could she want?"
"I was just saying ..."
The woman turns back to me and tightens her grip.

"So 'Havva,' she says, that's my name, Havva, 'Havva, this Arab guy is bothering me. I'm afraid to go in the elevator, afraid to go alone to the bathroom.' And I say, 'That's awful!' But I tell her, 'Don't worry, I know exactly what to do.' Right away I knew what to do."

"You didn't know right away. You asked me when I got home," her husband says.

She shoots him a frozen smile. "I knew right away."
Ilana manages somehow to block out the conversation and concentrate on the music. "*Wala shaf elkalb kablak farhah wahdah,*" she sings softly in my ear, together with the soloist. "My heart never knew happiness before you, my heart never knew anything in life but the taste of pain and suffering!"

"You have to know what works with them," the woman says, pointing with her chin at the man two rows before us. "We have a nephew who's an infantry battalion commander in the reserves."

"Two falafels," her husband says, tapping his shoulder. "He knows Gabi Ashkenazi personally."

"So I'm on the land line with Hadas and I call Ze'ev on my cell phone. He's at work but I tell him, Ze'ev, go straight home, put on your uniform, strap on your pistol, and head over to VAT. Invite Hadas down to the cafeteria for coffee."

"Did she say when Ya'akov is coming home?" the man wonders. "I don't understand the boy. He shouldn't leave his wife stranded like that. I never did."

"He called, don't you remember? He was delayed."

"*Hat a'inaik tisrah fi dounyethum a'ineyyah!*" The singer looks heavenward. "Bring your eyes close so that my eyes can get lost in the life of your eyes! Bring your hands so that my hands will rest in the touch of your hands!"

"Ze'ev's a great guy, always ready to help," the husband assures me.

"So he does just what I say, and in half an hour, he's on the tenth floor at VAT escorting Hadas down to the cafeteria on floor three for a coffee."

"So they get on the elevator," the husband said.

"And who's there? Guess?"

I look at the man two rows before us, is holding his arms up high, waving them to the beat, but also as if he wants to grab the singer on the stage.

"Him?"

"Precisely," the woman says. "And there's Hadas with this army officer in uniform, with his rank, and his pistol on his hip."

"Do you think he gets up close?" the man asks me.

"He retreats into the farthest corner he can find," the woman chortles.

"*Mina el wujud w'iba'idni*," Ilana intoned in my right ear. The plump woman from Tarshiha continues the line: "Take me away from the universe, Far away, far away. Me, and you, far away, far away. Alone."

"So you know what happens?" the woman asks.

"There's an earthquake!" the man says.

I twitch. "An earthquake?"

The woman looks at the singer. "Not as if. A real earthquake."

"Last week," the man explains. "You probably didn't feel it, but the VAT building, it's one of those new buildings built to be flexible. So the whole building starts to sway."

"And that Arab, he gets propelled from the corner where he's cowering straight at Hadas and Ze'ev," the woman says. "Thrown right into their arms."

"So there he is, embracing this religious woman and this army officer," the man says, chuckling. "Ya'akov should have seen them." Then he adds mournfully: "I wish Ya'akov would come home already."

The woman continued: "He looks at her, and then at him, and there's terror in his eyes. That's what Hadas says. And they reach the third floor, and before the door's even half open, he bolts out of there. And in the week since, he's made sure not to get anywhere near Hadas."

Um Kulthum of the north builds up to a climax as she comes to the end of the song. "*Omri dhayea' yehsibuh izay a'alaya? Inta Omri illi ibtada b'nurak sabahuh!* How could they consider that part of my life? You are my life that dawns with your light!"

As the sound of the orchestra fades, a few seconds of utter silence fill the room; the audience is too moved to react. Then the applause breaks out. Gradually, by twos and threes and then by whole rows, people rise, joining the already standing man two rows in front of us. The woman finally loosens her grip on me as she and her husband, and Ilana and I, stand in awe of the orchestra.

Ilana leans over to speak to her.

"And there he is?" she says, directing her gaze at the man two rows in front.

Her husband is looking at him warily, uncertainly, in trepidation.

"There he is," the woman says.

And her husband repeats after her: "There he is."

The Truth About Dave

I think it was during my senior year in high school that my friend Dave discovered the truth, and since I was his best friend, Dave was determined that I should know the truth as well.

It was a cover story in, I'm pretty sure, *Time* magazine, that set Dave off. A big spread about the Shroud of Turin, a cloth that many Christians believe bears an image of the crucified Jesus. New research, the magazine reported, proved that the cloth and the image dated from the first century A.D.

"Wow," Dave said, putting the magazine down and digging into the chocolate ice cream I'd dished out to him in my family's kitchen. "We all gotta become Christians now!"

"Ha," I said. Dave had, after all, been in my Hebrew school carpool. His Mom made a mean kugel and his older sister was going out with the son of the military attaché at the Israeli embassy.

"I'm serious," Dave said. "It says here that it's Jesus on the shroud. That means you have to believe in him."

I grabbed his arm because I was afraid he was about to mark an ice cream cross on his chest. "I don't know, Dave. How can you be so sure? But let's say they're right. How do you get from that to the catechism?"

"What's a catechism?" Dave wrestled his arm free and stuffed more Ben & Jerry's into his maw.

For four months, he wouldn't let me alone. He told me how he'd been born again and how he was going to heaven and that only the grace of Jesus could save me. Look, he was my friend, so I listened patiently and tried to calm my Mom down and explain that Dave was just going through a phase.

Since Dave and I were best buddies, we went off to college together. College changes people, and after a week, I noticed Dave had stopped kneeling by his bed each night to say his prayers. He stopped shaving and he started growing out his hair.

"The assassination of Salvador Allende by the nefarious forces of world capitalist oppression," he told me, "proves that Mao was right. The march of history moves only in one direction. The peasants and downtrodden will stride on to ultimate victory and all those who oppose them—indeed, all those who do not join them—will be consigned to the trash bin of history. It is time for you to follow me into the Workers World Party!"

"We're in college," I told him. "The only parties that interest me are ones with girls."

But it was no good. I was his best friend and he did not want to enter the socialist paradise without me. He plied me with pamphlets and dragged me to demonstrations. It seemed like we couldn't have a conversation in which Trotsky was not mentioned. It was annoying at times, but what are friends for, if not to serve as sounding boards for what you have on your mind? I tried to be a good listener.

"Why can't you accept the truth?" he sometimes shouted in frustration.

"Well, you know, I tend to be skeptical. To see the other side of every question."

Ultimately, though, Russians with beards couldn't compete with Katrina, a slender Danish exchange student whom Dave found one afternoon on the quad, standing behind the booklet-laden table next to his. Dave tried to cure her of false consciousness, but in the end, it was he who switched tables, from Workers World to EST.

"It'll change your life," he insisted, his face very close to mine, at the EST guest seminar he organized in our room. "It'll transform your ability to experience living so that the situations you've been trying to change or put up with clear up just in the process of life itself!"

He was holding a pen and a form that asked for four hundred bucks in exchange for spending an entire day locked in a hotel conference room with a guy yelling at me.

"I kind of like my life as it is," I demurred. "Anyway, I don't have the money. I guess I'll just have to wait around for the thing I'm putting up with to clear up in the process of life itself."

"I am so disappointed in you. Four hundred dollars is nothing when you get the truth in return."

On the day we graduated, Katrina jilted Dave and ran off with a Scientology practitioner. Dave's parents, who were desperate to get their truth-hungry son on track, offered the two of us a free trip to Israel. So we stuffed a few pairs of jeans into our backpacks and set off for a kibbutz in the desert.

"At worst, the goyim want to kill us," said Avner, the reserve paratrooper major who went out with us to set up sprinklers in the cotton fields. "At best, they won't lift a finger to help us. Israel is the only hope for Jewish survival. And if we die here, at least we die with honor, after fighting with everything we've got."

Back on our cots, Dave turned to me and said, "You know, what Avner said is really true."

"Uh-oh," I said.

"We've got to make aliya. It's our responsibility to the Jewish people. And serve in the IDF, in the toughest and most dangerous unit we can get into. Are you with me?"

"I don't know. I've just been here one day."

"A single day is sufficient to learn the truth," Dave said.

I really wanted to go home at the end of that summer, but Dave wouldn't hear of it. So I went with him to the Ministry of Absorption and signed up to be Israeli. His motivation: Zionism. Mine: to get Dave to shut up.

Once he became Israeli, David realized that Zionist truth came in several flavors. He started out as a committed Labor Zionist, then a devout advocate of Greater Israel. Then he decided that the true Zionist message was one of unity and he became a radical proponent of a series of movements whose truth lay in their commitment to the premise that all other Zionist truths really meant the same thing—Dash, Shinui, the Third Way and then the Center party.

Whatever it was, he wouldn't leave me alone. Whatever party he was in was the only one that could save Israel and the Jewish people. He spared no effort to force me to agree with him. Look, he was my friend, so I listened as politely as I could.

It was when he was canvassing votes at the Western Wall one Friday afternoon that he was picked up by Meir, the eternal Jew who has for the last two millennia set up Shabbat meals at the Kotel. Meir's sharp eye immediately saw that Dave was a truth seeker, a promising receptacle for the Holy Fire.

On Sunday, Dave enrolled in Aish HaTorah.

"All God's truth is in these books," Dave said when I visited him at the yeshiva in the Old City. "There's no need for any others."

"Hey, Dave, I know, but it's not for me," I said.

"Stop resisting. Conquer your evil impulse. You always are so full of questions. Torah is the answer."

"But I can't help being skeptical."

"I feel so sorry for you," he said. "The truth lies within reach and you turn your back on it."

Not that turning my back helped. Dave barraged me with invitations to classes and lectures. He signed me up for newsletters and had unctuous rabbis telephone me late at night.

After all these years, it started getting to me.

"Dave," I said to him one Friday afternoon when he was trying to drag me to his house for a Shabbat dinner. "Could you, well, maybe give me a break?"

He dropped my arm in astonishment.

"Give you a break? But you're my friend! How can I leave you in the dark when I've seen the light?"

"Doesn't friendship mean accepting me as I am and not trying to change me into something else?"

"How ungrateful! Don't you understand what I've tried to do for you? My entire life has been devoted to saving you from eternal damnation, from suffering the fate of an egg broken to make the omelet of the proletarian revolution, from the angst of postindustrial existential crisis, from assimilation and a second Holocaust, from the perils of extremism, and from a life cut off from God. And you claim that I'm insensitive? If that's how you feel, go off and live your benighted life as you wish. Just don't come running to me when you miss the bus to ultimate redemption!"

Dave and I weren't friends any more. I suppose I was sad about that, but to tell you the truth, it was a relief to be able to find my own way through life without someone nagging me all the time.

Still, when my Android rang last week, it was great to hear Dave's voice again.

"Hey, I owe you an apology," he said. "I realize that you were right all along. Truth is elusive. Texts are indeterminate. Values are relative. We can only grope our way through the universe blindly."

"Oh, Dave," I said. "What is it now?"

"Don't you understand? Postmodernism is the answer."

"Are you sure?"

"Of course not!" Dave said, and I thought for a moment that he really had changed.

"That's great, Dave. I'm so happy that you've come to grips with uncertainty."

"No question about it!" My heart fell. I knew that tone of voice. "I'm absolutely convinced of it and here's why you should be, too."

Fireflies

Fireflies, forgotten for many years, reappear one summer evening.

Shabbat, Riverside Park, along the Hudson. Under the shelter of tall trees, runners race by. Couples stroll, families with small children sprawl on the grass. The first flashes, as the sun drops low over New Jersey, catch me by surprise. Then the tears begin.

It is like a dream. Niot's look of pure delight and wonder when he sees fireflies for the first time. He is twelve years old, or perhaps ten. We are in Silver Spring, at my parents' home. I am sitting in an armchair reading a newspaper. Twilight falls. Niot appears behind the frame of the large sliding glass door that separates the family room from the backyard. He catches my eye, then turns his gaze to the yard. Points of weightless brilliance as day slides into night.

"Specks of living light / twinkling in the dark," Tagore calls them. The picture is clear and present to me in the park at dusk, as clear as if I were again in that armchair and Niot beyond the sliding door.

When Niot first began to appear in my dreams, he was far away, visible for an instant, then gone. I wept in my sleep.

How could light make me cry? How could a creature showing itself to the world make me feel that world as empty? The firefly's light is a cold light. It startles but it does not warm.

Winged embers mark trails along the river, like comets flying close to the sun, tails aimed at me.

Perhaps only I see them? Runners lope by with buds in their ears, bikers swerve, unperturbed by the orbs. The gazes of families focus inward, are not drawn out. Here and there a toddler points a finger, reaches out, and then, hopes disappointed, turns back to those he loves.

Aloft in daylight, a firefly has no soul. It is nothing if not seen.

I do not see Niot on the evening when I am sure I will, soon after he died. I am on my way to meet my family at a café. Suddenly, some steps from home, a certainty overwhelms me: Niot will be there, too. His accident, the day and a half in intensive care, the harvest of his organs—all that was staged. A farce, a test, an illusion, a dream. He will laugh at my gullibility.

I know it cannot be, but am no less confident for that knowledge. When I arrive at the café, he is not there.

The firefly flies longer than it shines.

***

Later, Niot stays for longer. Twice or three times I touch him.

I sit in a cab, squeezed between Niot and his brother. His body presses up against mine. He laughs, a laugh that I hear and also feel as it courses through his body. I put my arm around him and bring his head close to me. Then I wake up.

As the sun disappears behind Hoboken, the lightning bugs illuminate the night. The walkers on the paths fade; the trees blend into the darkness. The night weighs heavily; on the streets and highways demons clatter and roar, the muffled cries of pandemonium. Are these spectral beetles not the lesser terror? But you cannot navigate by their light, nor can one follow the phantoms. They lead in all directions.

I and several other people are in a long, narrow room with two sets of bunk beds on either side, as in a youth hostel. A woman speaks—she is a teacher, but also a doctor. Niot is in a drawer under the bottom bunk of one of the beds. The woman strides over and tries to open the drawer, but cannot because the opposite bed blocks it. I offer to push the offending bed aside, but she keeps pulling. I tell her it is no use, Niot is dead. "You are not the person to determine that," she informs me. Finally, contorting herself, she manages to yank the drawer open. Niot lies there. She examines him and pronounces: "He'll come out of it." Niot has many bruises. He opens his eyes and asks: "Abba, when will I be able to get out?" I weep, go on my knees to embrace him and tell him how much we all miss him. Then I wake up.

I try to flee. I find a path that ascends to the world above, but it is steeper than it looks in the dark and I cannot climb. My strength gone, I sit on the grass and fireflies flit around me. Such are souls in Hades. Not even heroes or musicians can retrieve them. Sometimes they are called shades, but here they are sparks.

Philosophers speak sometimes of the spark of life. But life is not a flash, a flicker, a glimmer, a glint. You do not just see it in the dark. It is felt, it touches, it sounds, it smells. Is this not how we tell the fantasies of the night from the truths of the day? In dreams we most often only see and hear, seldom smell or taste, only sometimes touch. The touch of one's child's body is more real than truth. If it is in a dream, the dream is real in a way that much is not.

Sitting in the park, I swipe a firefly out of the air. But you cannot touch a firefly. In the hand, it disappoints. It crawls, it flutters; soft and small, it hardly seems alive. Nothing of the warmth and weight of his body against mine. Better to free it and dream.

***

I rise and return to the path. Fireflies dart across it, blocking my way. A couple, holding hands and deep in conversation, passes me in the dusk. They are not deterred. I brave the bugs, the blinking luminescence of the dark. Is that not what laughter is?

Niot's laugh lit up many a darkness. He laughed naturally, frequently, at jokes, at pretenses, at the foibles of others, at himself. A rolling laugh that twinkled for seconds, faded, and then burst again into light. Perhaps when laughs die they become fireflies of a summer evening, flaring after sundown.

A biker, braking, rolls past me. In recent dreams, Niot keeps a middle distance. Just a few weeks ago, in the midst of a long saga dealing with other matters entirely, he suddenly appears. There he is in our home, wearing shorts, looking as he did in high school. I am delighted to see him, but I have to go out to deal with my dream affairs. I also realize that Niot's presence is a mistake. He is not supposed to be here and, sooner or later, the error will be noticed and he will be gone.

I ask him what his plans are and he says noncommittally that he doesn't have any. I think to myself that, obviously, it is difficult for him to plan because he does not know when he will be dead again. And I realize that, when that happens, I and the family will have to mourn again all over from the start, and the thought is too painful to bear. I am caught at the door. Niot is right there before me, but more than an arm's reach away.

The path winds, switching back on itself as it ascends. I hear the heavy breathing of a runner who soon passes me from behind. The hubbub of the city grows louder. Out of the corner of my eye I see a traffic light change from red to green. Before the final climb to the street I turn around and look between the trees. The air-fires are fewer; twilight, their time to shine, is nearly over. The souls return to their burrows, their shelter behind the bark of maples and beeches. I hear the shouts of boys playing basketball and the whine of a small child. But my tears are gone, I no longer weep, I have a destination and much to do. A few final steps and Niot is no longer close. He is nearby, always nearby, but more than an arm's reach away.

Niot, on the far side of a glass door, pointing in happy astonishment at flying radiance.

"I leave no trace of wings in the air / but I am glad I have had my flight," says the poet.

Sometimes a firefly burns for twenty years before going out.

Plane Story

The air is unexpectedly cool and damp for early September when I emerge from Terminal 3 and cross over to the Air Train. I'm alone and there are no human sounds, only the roar of traffic on the highway. Even that is muted as the elevator door shuts.

I look up from 60C on my Delta flight from JFK to TLV. A pudgy young guy in a white shirt and a beard is standing over me.

"I've got the window," he says apologetically.

I snap my laptop shut and squiggle out of my aisle seat.

"Sorry. You were writing something," he says.

"It's ok."

He squeezes past me with a hat box and a large plastic bag full of cookies. He places them on 60B.

"I saw at the desk that no one's sitting here," he explains. He points at my computer. "Work?"

"Yes," I say. "A story. I have a column in a magazine and the deadline is coming up. I'm just trying to get it started before takeoff."

"Well, don't let me bother you. By the way, I'm Yehuda."

"Haim. Thanks. Actually, I'm not sure if I want to write it."

I settle back into my seat, pull down the tray table, and reopen the laptop. I tap out:

'Stand clear of the closing doors, please,' I hear Niot intone, a broad smile on his face. The door opens and I walk down the corridor to the platform.

Last February, this space was not silent and I was not on my own. I'd arrived in the early morning from Israel with Niot and his two sisters, all of us on our way to a family reunion. He'd chain-chugged Coke the whole flight and was in high spirits.

Suddenly the seat in front of me pivots back, nearly crushing my screen and pushing the computer so close to my body that further typing is impossible. I look up and see a black cloth kipah. A loud voice emerges from below it:

"Steward! Steward! Where's my blanket! Look, he's not listening to me."

This last sentence is directed at the red-haired young man sitting across the aisle, who is talking up the young woman sitting behind him. The figure under the kipah—he has a bushy beard and intense eyes—leans into the aisle.

"I'm Shmuel," he said at high volume. "Who're you?"

"Oh, hi," the young man said. "I'm Nadav." He speaks English well, but with a notable Israeli accent. Unlike most of the other men sitting in our vicinity, his head is uncovered.

"Nadav!" Shmuel proclaims. "Do you know who Nadav was?"

"He was a king of Israel," Nadav says.

"A king of Israel!" Shmuel exclaims. "I never heard of a Nadav who was king of Israel." He pushes himself up from his chair and surveys the passengers in the back section of the airplane, as if to ask if any had heard of this King Nadav.

"Sure," says Nadav. "Not for very long, though. Just a couple years."

"I don't know about that Nadav," says Shmuel. "I was thinking of Nadav, the son of Aharon, the high priest. Do you know about that Nadav?"

A steward passes between them and asks Shmuel to return his seat to the upright position for takeoff and to keep his voice down as other passengers are trying to sleep.

"All right, all right," says Shmuel. "Tell me." He leans far over until he looks Nadav directly in the eye. "What do you do?"

"I'm studying biology at Ben-Gurion University. I just spent the summer working in a lab at MIT. We've developed a method for tracking the degradation of proteins in bacteria."

I power off my laptop and take out my copy of *Wuthering Heights*.

Yehuda stops chatting in Yiddish with the yeshiva student behind us and turns to me.

"Is that—waddayoucallit—fiction?" The plane speeds down the runway.

"Yes, it's a famous mid-nineteenth century novel about good and evil, set in northern England."

"Once I tried reading a novel," Yehuda says as the plane tilts up into the air. "My brother gave me the first Harry Potter book and said that I had to read it. I got through the first few chapters and it was pretty good. But I really prefer reading about real things. You know, history, science, that kind of stuff."

I glance at Nadav, who is displaying far more forbearance than I would for the lecture he is receiving from his neighboring Habadnik.

"Nadav and Avihu were the sons of Aharon, the high priest of Israel," Shmuel tells him. "They had the great privilege of serving God in the Holy Tabernacle. They could enter the holy precincts and make sacrifices. But what happened to them? The Torah tells us 'vayakrivu lifnei Hashem esh zara,' they offered a foreign fire before God. And then God killed them. Really. That's exactly what happened. But why would God kill these two guys who were bringing him an offering? Why would they offer a foreign fire when they are privileged to be so close to God? You know what the Or HaHayyim says? You know the Or HaHayyim?"

"Tell me," says Nadav.

"The Or HaHayyim was Rabbi Haim ben Atar, a Moroccan who came to Jerusalem and was one of the great commentators on the Torah. He reminds us that the word for sacrifice, 'yakrivu,' also means 'close.' Nadav was so close to God that he was already worthy of the next world. So God took him and his brother. His father,

Aharon, was sad, of course, but he did not say a word. He understood that his sons had reached a higher level of holiness than even he, the high priest, had."

"You don't say." Nadav is more than just polite. "Interesting story."

"Real stuff, when you read it, you know it is real," Yehuda explains to me. "But when you read fiction, it's not real, so why should you read it?"

"I read a lot of non-fiction, too," I tell Yehuda. "But I think there are things we can get from made-up stories that we can't get from non-fiction."

"Like what?"

"Well, you enter into other people, their minds, and the way they use language. Fiction gives you a chance to consider how your life might be if you lived in a different place, in a different time, or under different circumstances. Also, stories bring home to us that we live within language and that the way we speak and write affects the way we see the world. Each story we read reminds us that we can tell our own stories in hundreds of different ways."

"Ok," says Yehuda.

"You've studied Torah, so that idea should be familiar to you," I say. "Take any story from the Bible or the Rabbis. Take, say, the story of David and his son Avshalom."

"But that's a true story," Yehduda says.

"So say it's true. Even so, the story was written using a particular structure, and with particular words. The same story could be told in lots of different ways, but it was written in this particular way. So when we study the book, we need to ask, like our commentators always do, why these words were chosen and not some other words."

Yehuda thinks this over. "Tell me more about the novel you're reading."

"Well, one thing that's intriguing about it is the way it's told. There is a narrator who tells us the story as he hears it from a servant woman, who in turn includes things she has heard from yet other characters. I'm pondering why the author decided to tell the story in such an indirect way. She could, after all, have simply told the story in her own voice."

"I don't know much about the Bible, but we learned some in school," Nadav tells Shmuel. "And I seem to remember learning that one interpretation is that Aharon's sons were killed because they thought none of the available women were good enough for them."

"That's also true," says Shmuel. "I think that that appears in the Holy Zohar. You know the story of the Holy Zohar? How it was written by Rabbi Shimon bar Yochai?"

"Still," Yehuda insists, "I like to read about real things, like history."

"Why are there so many books about, say, World War II?" I ask him. "Why do people keep writing books about it? If there were just one real story about the war, we'd only need one book. Historians would long ago have said all there was to say about what happened."

"I never thought of it that way," Yehuda says. "So it's like Talmud. You keep studying, and each time you study it, you understand it in new ways."

"Right. Take this conversation. When you recount it to someone tomorrow, think of how many ways you could tell it."

"Wasn't the Zohar written in the Middle Ages in Spain?" Nadav asks.

"It was revealed to us then," says Shmuel. "But it was actually given by God to Moses and written down later by Rabbi Shimon bar Yochai. There are truths you don't learn at Ben-Gurion University. Now tell me about these bacteria of yours. What's wrong with their proteins?"

"But I'm keeping you from writing your story," Yehuda apologizes. "What kind of story is it?"

"A sad one," I say. "About my son. He died five months ago."

"I'm so sorry," Yehuda says. "I should let you write."

"I don't think I can," I reply. "Not this one, anyway."

Over the loudspeaker a steward asks us to close the windows and turn off the lights so the passengers can sleep through the New York night and into the European morning. Shmuel tips his chair back again, Yehuda dons a neck pillow, I wrap myself in a red airplane blanket, and Nadav puts his head down on his tray table.

About four hours later, I'm the first to wake up. I stand up, stretch, go to the lavatory, then take out my tallit and tefillin and recite my morning prayers. Afterward, as I wrap up my phylacteries and fold my prayer shawl, Nadav stirs, and we chat briefly about his research. I sit down with my book. Shmuel stretches and says a general good morning to everyone around him.

Nadav looks behind him. The girl is still sleeping. He leans over to Shmuel.

"Hey," he says. "Tell me a story."

About the Author

Haim Watzman is the author of two previous books, *Company C: An American's Life as a Citizen-Soldier in Israel* and *A Crack in the Earth: A Journey Up Israel's Rift Valley*, the latter a finalist for the Sami Rohr Prize in Jewish Literature. He has also translated many important Israeli books by some of the country's leading journalists, scholars, and writers—among them David Grossman, Tom Segev, Amos Oz, and Shlomo Avineri—and he edited Yuval Noah Harari's bestselling *Sapiens*. His fiction and essays appear regularly in his "Necessary Stories" column in *The Jerusalem Report*. He lives in Jerusalem. More stories, and additional information on this book, can be found on his website, southjerusalem.com.

About the Illustrator

Israeli illustrator Avi Katz's art has accompanied Haim Watzman's stories in The Jerusalem Report since 2008. Katz was born in Philadelphia and immigrated to Israel in 1970, where he graduated the Bezalel Academy of Art. He has created thousands of magazine illustrations and almost 200 children's books; which have been recognized with a National Jewish Book Award and other honors.

www.ingramcontent.com/pod-product-compliance
Lightning Source LLC
Chambersburg PA
CBHW070308120726
47910CB00007B/2400